Falling in with Fortune; Or, The Experiences of a Young Secretary

By

Jr. Horatio Alger, Edward Stratemeyer

Falling in with Fortune; Or, The Experiences of a Young Secretary

by **Jr. Horatio Alger, Edward Stratemeyer**

Copyright © 2023

All Rights reserved.
No part of this publication may be reproduced, stored in a retrieval system, or transmitted in any form or by any means, electronic, mechanical, photocopying or Otherwise, without the written permission of the publisher.

The author/editor asserts the moral right to be identified as the author/editor of this work.

ISBN: 978-93-57273-01-5

Published by

DOUBLE 9 BOOKS

2/13-B, Ansari Road, Daryaganj
New Delhi – 110002
info@double9books.com
www.double9books.com
Tel. 011-40042856

This book is under public domain

ABOUT THE AUTHOR

Author Horatio Alger Jr. was born in Chelsea, Massachusetts, a coastal New England town, on January 13, 1832. He was the son of Olive Augusta Fenno and Horatio Alger Sr., a Unitarian pastor. On July 18, 1899, he passed away at his sister's house in Natick, Massachusetts. His passing was almost unnoticed. In the Glenwood Cemetery in South Natick, Massachusetts, he is buried in the family plot.

American publisher, children's book author, and creator of the Stratemeyer Syndicate Edward L. Stratemeyer. was born in Elizabeth, New Jersey, the sixth child and youngest of Henry Julius Stratemeyer and Anna Siegel. In 1890, Stratemeyer relocated to Newark, New Jersey, and started a paper business. He continued to compose articles under aliases while running his business. On March 25, 1891, he wed Magdalena Van Camp, a businessman's daughter from Newark. The pair had two daughters who would eventually lead the Stratemeyer Syndicate: Harriet Stratemeyer Adams (1892-1982) and Edna C. Squier (1895-1974).

CONTENTS

PREFACE. 7

CHAPTER I. – THROWN OUT OF EMPLOYMENT. 8

CHAPTER II. – THE ACCUSATION, AND WHAT FOLLOWED 14

CHAPTER III. – GETTING SETTLED. 19

CHAPTER IV. – THE OLD SECRETARY AND THE NEW. 25

CHAPTER V. – A PLOT AGAINST ROBERT 31

CHAPTER VI. – MRS. VERNON'S MONEY. 35

CHAPTER VII. – THE DOCTOR'S VISIT. 38

CHAPTER VIII. – FREDERIC VERNON'S PERPLEXITY 43

CHAPTER IX. – ROBERT REACHES LONDON. 48

CHAPTER X. – MATTERS AT HOME. 53

CHAPTER XI. – VERNON MAKES ANOTHER MOVE. 58

CHAPTER XII. – AN UNEXPECTED RESULT. 62

CHAPTER XIII. – VERNON'S HIGH-HANDED PROCEEDINGS. 67

CHAPTER XIV. – VERNON'S UNWELCOME VISITOR. 72

CHAPTER XV. – A FIGHT AND A FIRE. 76

CHAPTER XVI. – ROBERT SHOWS HIS BRAVERY. 82

CHAPTER XVII. – A DIAMOND SCARFPIN. 87

CHAPTER XVIII. – VERNON PLAYS THE PENITENT. 92

CHAPTER XIX. – MRS. VERNON'S BANK ACCOUNT. 97

CHAPTER XX. — THE RUNAWAY ALONG THE CLIFF. 102

CHAPTER XXI. — THE CABLEGRAM FROM CHICAGO. 107

CHAPTER XXII. — FARMER PARSONS' STORY. 112

CHAPTER XXIII. — AUNT AND NEPHEW'S AGREEMENT. 117

CHAPTER XXIV. — THE ATTACK IN THE STATEROOM. 122

CHAPTER XXV. — A FRIEND IN NEED. 127

CHAPTER XXVI. — IN CHICAGO ONCE MORE 132

CHAPTER XXVII. — DICK MARDEN'S GOOD NEWS. 137

CHAPTER XXVIII. — IN WHICH MRS. VERNON IS MISSING 142

CHAPTER XXIX. — DOCTOR RUSHWOOD'S SANITARIUM. 147

CHAPTER XXX. — FREDERIC VERNON'S DEMANDS 152

CHAPTER XXXI. — ROBERT DECIDES TO ACT. 157

CHAPTER XXXII. — THE BEGINNING OF THE END. 162

CHAPTER XXXIII. — ROBERT'S HEROISM--CONCLUSION. 168

PREFACE.

"Falling in with Fortune" is a complete tale in itself, but forms the second of two companion volumes, the first being entitled, "Out for Business."

In this story are related the adventures of Robert Frost, who figured in the other volume mentioned. In the first tale we saw how Robert was compelled to leave home on account of the harsh actions of his step-father, and what he did while "out for business," as he frequently expressed it.

In the present tale our hero, by a curious combination of circumstances, becomes the private secretary to a rich lady, and travels with this lady to England and other places. The lady has a nephew whose character is none of the best, and as this young man had formerly occupied the position now assigned to Robert, our hero's place becomes no easy one to fill. Yet his natural stoutheartedness helps him to overcome every obstacle and brings his many surprising adventures to a satisfactory ending.

The two stories, "Out for Business" and "Falling in with Fortune," give to the reader the last tales begun by that famous writer of boys' tales, Mr. Horatio Alger, Jr., whose books have sold to the extent of hundreds of thousands of copies, not alone in America, but likewise in England, Australia, and elsewhere. The gifted writer was stricken when on the point of finishing the tales, and when he saw that he could not complete them himself, it was to the present writer that he turned, and an outline for a conclusion was drawn up which met with his approval--and this outline had been filled out in order to bring the stories to a finish and make them, as nearly as possible, what Mr. Alger intended they should be. The success of the first of the companion tales causes the present writer to hope that the second will meet with equal favor.

Arthur M. Winfield.

July 1, 1900.

CHAPTER I.
THROWN OUT OF EMPLOYMENT.

"A telegram for you, Robert."

"A telegram for me?" repeated Robert Frost, as he took the envelope which his fellow clerk, Livingston Palmer, handed him. "I wonder where it can be from?"

"Perhaps it's from your mother. Your step-father may be sick again, and she may want you at home."

"No, Mr. Talbot is quite well now; my mother said so in her letter of yesterday. I imagine this is from Timberville, Michigan."

"Is your friend, Dick Marden, still up there attending to that lumber business for his uncle?"

"Yes."

"Didn't he want you to stay there with him?"

"He did, but I told him I would rather remain in the city. I like working for Mr. Gray, here in the ticket office, a great deal better than I do lumbering."

"I can see that. You are an out and out business boy, Robert. I shouldn't be surprised some day to see you have a cut-rate ticket office of your own."

"I'd rather be in a bank, or some large wholesale house, Livingston. But excuse me while I read the telegram."

"Certainly. Don't mind me."

Tearing open the envelope, Robert Frost pulled out the bit of yellow paper, upon which was written the following:

> "I am called away to California and to Canada on business. May remain for three months. Will write to you later on. My uncle's case is in a bad mix-up again.

"Dick Marden."

Robert read the brief communication with much interest. Dick Marden was much older than the boy, but a warm friendship existed between the pair.

"No bad news, I hope," said Livingston Palmer, after waiting on a customer, who had come in to buy a cut-rate ticket to Denver.

"Dick Marden has gone to California. He says the Amberton claim to that timber land is in a bad mix-up again."

"I see. Well, that doesn't concern you, does it?"

"Not exactly. But I would like to see Mr. Amberton come out ahead on the deal, for I think he deserves it."

"I know you worked hard enough to get that map for him," said Livingston Palmer, laughing. "Have you ever heard anything more of those two rascals who tried to get the map away from you?"

"No--and I don't want to hear from them. All I want is to be left alone, to make my own way in the world," concluded Robert.

Robert Frost was a lad of sixteen, strongly built, and with a handsome, expressive face. He had been born and brought up in the village of Granville, some fifty or sixty miles from Chicago, but had left his home several months before to do as he had just said, make his own way in the world.

The readers of the companion tale to this, "Out for Business," already know why Robert left home. To new readers I would state that it was on account of his step-father, James Talbot, who had married the widow Frost mainly for the purpose of getting possession of the fortune which had been left to her,--a fortune which upon her death was to go to her only child, Robert.

From his first entrance into the handsome and comfortable Frost homestead, James Talbot had acted very dictatorial toward Robert, and the boy, being naturally high-strung, had resented this, and many a bitter quarrel had ensued. At last Robert could stand his step-father's manner no longer, and, with his mother's consent, he left home for Chicago, to try his fortunes in the great city by the lakes.

Robert was fortunate in falling in with a rough but kind-hearted miner named Dick Marden, and the miner, who was well-to-do, obtained for the youth a position in the cut-rate ticket office of one

Peter Gray, an old acquaintance. Gray gave Robert first five and then seven dollars per week salary, and to this Marden added sufficient to make an even twelve dollars, so the boy was enabled to live quite comfortably.

Dick Marden had an uncle living at Timberville, Michigan, who was old and feeble, and who was having a great deal of trouble about some timber lands which he claimed, but which an Englishman and a French Canadian were trying to get away from him. There was a map of the lands in the possession of an old lumberman named Herman Wenrich, and his daughter Nettie, who lived in Chicago, and this map Robert obtained for Marden and his uncle, Felix Amberton, and delivered it to them, although not until he had had several encounters with the people who wished to keep the map from Amberton. For his services Robert was warmly thanked by both Amberton and Marden, and the lumberman promised to do the handsome thing by the boy as soon as his titles to the lumber lands were clearly established in law.

During the time spent in Chicago Robert had had considerable trouble with his step-father, who was trying his best to get hold of some of Mrs. Talbot's money, with the ostensible purpose of going into the real estate business in the great city of the lakes. But a stroke of paralysis had placed Mr. Talbot on a sick bed, and upon his recovery he had told both his wife and his step-son that he intended to turn over a new leaf. Mrs. Talbot believed him, but Robert was suspicious, for he felt that his step-father's nature was too utterly mean for him to reform entirely.

"I hope he does reform, mother," the boy said to his fond parent. "But if I were you I would not expect too much--at least, at the start. I would not trust him with my money."

"He has not asked me for money," had been Mrs. Talbot's reply.

"But he wanted that ten thousand dollars to open up with in Chicago."

"That was before he had the attack of paralysis, Robert."

"He may want it again, as soon as he is himself once more. Take my advice and be careful what you do." And so mother and son parted, not to see each other again for a long while. But Robert was right; less than two months later James Talbot applied again for the money, stating that he would be very careful of it, so that not a dollar should be lost. He thought himself a keen business man, but thus far he had allowed every dollar that had come into his possession to slip through his fingers.

Robert felt sorry that Dick Marden had gone to California, for he had reckoned on seeing his friend upon his return to Chicago.

"Now, I suppose I won't see him for a long while," he thought.

Robert had settled down at the office, expecting the position to be a permanent one, but on the Saturday following the receipt of Marden's telegram a surprise awaited him. Mr. Gray called him into his private office.

"Robert," he said, "I have bad news for you."

"Bad news, Mr. Gray? What is it?"

"I am sorry to say it, but I shall have to dispense with your services from to-night."

Robert flushed, and felt dismayed. This announcement was like a thunderbolt from a clear sky.

"Are you dissatisfied with me, Mr. Gray?" he asked.

"Not at all. Your services have been entirely satisfactory."

"Then why do you send me away?"

"I cannot very well help it. I have a nephew from the country who wants a place in the city. His father has written me, asking as a favor that I will give Donald a place in my office. He is poor, and I don't see how I can refuse his request."

"Yes, sir, I see. I am glad you are not discharging me on account of dissatisfaction."

"You may be assured of that. I suppose you have some money saved up?"

"Yes, sir."

"And no doubt your friend Mr. Marden will provide for you?"

"Mr. Marden has gone to California for three months."

"But you know his address there?"

"No, sir."

Peter Gray looked sober, for he was a man of good feelings.

"Perhaps I can arrange to keep you," he said. "You know as much about the business as Mr. Palmer. I can discharge him and keep you."

"I would not consent to that, sir. Livingston Palmer needs his salary, and I wouldn't be willing to deprive him of it. I can get along somehow. When do you wish me to go?"

"My nephew arrived at my house this morning. He will be ready to go to work on Monday morning."

"Very well, sir."

"Of course I will give you a good recommendation--a first class one."

"Thank you, sir."

At six o'clock the broker handed Robert his week's wages, and Robert went out of the office, out of a place, and with prospects by no means flattering.

Fortunately for Robert he had about twenty dollars in his pocket, so that he was not in any immediate danger of suffering from want. He would have had more, but had bought some necessary articles of wearing apparel, assuming that his position was a permanent one.

Of course he began to seek for another place immediately. He examined the advertising columns of the daily papers, and inquired for anything he thought would suit him. But it so happened that business was unusually quiet, and he met with refusals everywhere, even where it was apparent that he was regarded favorably. There was one exception, however. He was offered three dollars a week in a small furnishing goods store, but this he felt that he could not afford to accept.

As he came back to his boarding place every afternoon, he grew more and more despondent.

"Is there no place open to me in this big city?" he asked himself.

One thing he was resolved upon. He would not go back to his old home. It would be too much of a triumph for his step-father, who had often predicted that Robert would fail in his undertaking to support himself. And yet he must do something.

He began to watch the newsboys near the Sherman House briskly disposing of their merchandise.

"I wonder if they make much," he thought.

He put the question to one pleasant-looking boy, of whom he bought an evening paper.

"I make about sixty or seventy cents a day," was the reply.

Sixty or seventy cents a day! That meant about four dollars a week. It was scarcely better than the salary offered in the furnishing goods store, and the employment would not be so agreeable. He felt that he should not like to have his step-father or any one who knew him in his native town seeing him selling daily papers in the street, so he decided not to take up that business except as a last resort.

One day he went into a large dry goods store to purchase a small article. He made his purchase and started to go out.

All at once he heard a cry, proceeding from a lady.

"I have lost my purse."

"That boy's got it!" said a voice.

Then much to his bewilderment Robert found himself seized by the shoulder, and a pocket-book was drawn out from the side pocket of his sack coat.

"Send for an officer!" said the floor-walker. "The boy is a thief!"

CHAPTER II.
THE ACCUSATION, AND WHAT FOLLOWED.

A person who is entirely innocent is likely to look confused when suddenly charged with theft. It came upon Robert so suddenly that he could not at first summon presence of mind enough to deny it. But at last he said indignantly, "I didn't take it. I never stole in my life."

"That's a likely story," said the floor-walker. "It got into your pocket itself, I suppose."

"I don't know how it got there. I only know I didn't put it there."

"Why did you come into the store--except to steal?"

"I came here to buy a necktie."

Just then in came an officer who had been summoned.

"Arrest that boy!" said the floor-walker. "He is a thief."

Robert started indignantly when the officer put his hand on his shoulder.

"That is false!" he said.

"Come along!" said the officer.

"Is there no one here who will speak for me?" asked Robert, looking about him on the suspicious and distrustful faces that surrounded him.

"Yes, I will do so," said a voice, and a tall, dignified looking gentleman with white hair pressed forward toward him.

All eyes were turned upon the gentleman.

"The boy is not a thief!" he said.

"Then perhaps," said the floor-walker sarcastically, "you can tell who is?"

"I can," returned the other calmly. "*There* is the thief!"

He pointed to a flashily attired young man who started to go out--protesting that it was all a mistake.

"That won't go down," said the floor-walker. "Who are you, sir, that try to screen the boy at the expense of an innocent man?"

"I am the Rev. Dr. Blank; I am pretty well known in Chicago, I believe."

This statement made a sensation. Some of those present recognized the clergyman, and even the floorwalker was impressed.

"Are you sure of this, sir?" he asked.

"Yes."

"Did you see the young man steal the pocket-book?"

"No, but I saw him put it into the boy's pocket."

By this time the policeman's attention had been called to the real thief.

"The minister is right, I make no doubt," he said. "I recognize that man. He is a well-known thief."

"Arrest him then!" said the floor-walker sullenly, for he was really sorry that Robert had been proven innocent.

The officer released his hold on our hero, and prepared to leave the store in charge of the real thief, who had, of course, emptied the pocket-book before placing it in Robert's pocket.

"Will you be present at the trial?" he asked the clergyman.

"Yes. There is my address. You can summon me."

"How can I thank you, sir?" said Robert warmly. "You have saved me from arrest."

"Thank God for that, my boy. I am glad that word of mine should do you such a service."

Robert walked out of the store feeling that he had had a very narrow escape. This was a relief, but it was quickly succeeded by anxious thoughts--for he was nearly out of money. His prospects were so uncertain that he blamed himself for incurring the expense of a necktie, though it had only cost him twenty-five cents.

Robert continued to seek for a position, but he seemed out of luck. Once he came near success. It was in a furnishing goods store. The shopkeeper seemed inclined to engage him, but before the decisive word was spoken his wife entered the store. She looked at Robert scrutinizingly.

"I think I have seen you before," she said sharply.

"I don't know, madam. I don't remember you."

"But I remember you. It was two days since. I saw you in a store on State Street. You were about to be arrested for stealing a wallet."

Robert blushed.

"Did you stay till it was discovered that someone else took it?" he asked.

"I know you got off somehow."

"I got off because I was innocent. I was as innocent as you were."

"Do you mean to insult me, boy?" asked the lady sharply.

"No, madam. I only say that I was innocent. It was shown that a man then in the store took the wallet. He was arrested, and I was released."

"Very likely he was a confederate of yours."

"If he had been he would have said so."

"At any rate, circumstances were very suspicious. Were you thinking of hiring this boy, William?"

"Yes, I liked his looks," answered the shopkeeper.

"Then be guided by me, and don't hire him."

"Why not? The charge seems to have been false."

"At any rate, he has been under suspicion. He can't be trusted."

"In that case," said Robert proudly, "I withdraw my application. I need the place enough, but if you are afraid to trust me I don't care to come."

"I am not afraid to trust you," said the owner of the shop kindly, "but my wife seems to have taken a prejudice against you."

"In that case I will go."

Robert bowed and left the store. His heart was full of disappointment and bitterness, and he resented the cruel want of consideration shown by the woman who had interfered between him and employment.

In fact, he had but fifteen cents left in his pocketbook. It was time for dinner, and he felt that he must eat. But where his next meal, outside of his boarding house, was to come from, he could not tell.

He was on State Street, and must go to another part of the city to find a cheap restaurant. He chanced to be passing the same store where he had almost suffered arrest.

"I wish I had never gone in there," he reflected. "It cost me a place."

As this thought passed through his mind a lady, richly dressed, passed through the portals of the store and stepped on the sidewalk.

Her glance rested on the boy.

"Didn't I see you in this store day before yesterday?" she asked.

"What!" thought Robert. "Does she remember me also?"

"I was here, madam," he replied.

"You were charged with stealing a wallet?"

"Yes, madam, but I hope you don't think that I did it."

"No; you were exonerated. But even if you had not been, I should know by your face that you were not a thief."

Robert brightened up.

"Thank you," he said gratefully. "I appreciate your confidence the more because I have just lost a place because a lady insisted that I might have been a confederate of the thief."

"Tell me about it. We will walk up the street, and you shall speak as we walk along."

Robert placed himself at her side, and told the story.

"Then you need employment?" she asked.

"Yes, madam. I need it very much. I have only fifteen cents left in my pocket."

"Do you live in the city?"

"I have been here only a short time. I came from the country."

"Are you well educated? Can you write a good hand? Are you good at figures?"

"I am nearly ready for college, but troubles at home prevented my going."

"You shall tell me of them later. Would you like to be my private secretary?"

"Yes, madam. I should feel very fortunate to procure such a position."

"Can you enter upon your duties at once?"

"Yes, madam."

"Then we will take a car, and you can accompany me home."

"Shall I go after my valise?"

"No, you can go after that this evening. If you accompany me now we shall be in time for dinner."

Rather dazed by the suddenness of his engagement, Robert hailed a passing car by direction of his companion, and they took seats. The ride proved to be a long one. They disembarked at Prairie Avenue, and the lady led the way to a handsome residence. Robert went up the front steps with her, and rang the bell.

The door was opened by a smart servant girl, who regarded Robert with some surprise.

"Is dinner ready, Martha?" asked the lady of the house.

"Yes, madam. It will be served at once."

"Take this young gentleman up to the back room on the third floor, so that he may prepare for dinner."

"Yes, Mrs. Vernon."

"You will find everything necessary for your toilet in the room which I have assigned you. By the way, what is your name?"

"Robert Frost."

"A good name. Martha will go up in ten minutes to conduct you to the dining room."

"If this is a dream," thought Robert, as he followed the servant upstairs--"it is a very pleasant one. I hope I shan't wake up till I have had dinner."

He was shown into a chamber of fair size, very handsomely furnished. Everything was at hand for making his toilet. Robert bathed his face and hands and combed his hair. He was quite ready when Martha knocked at the door.

"Dinner is served," she said. "I will show you the way to the dining room."

CHAPTER III.
GETTING SETTLED.

Robert was well prepared by long abstinence to do justice to the choice viands that were set before him. He had not been brought up in poverty, yet he had not been accustomed to the luxurious table maintained by Mrs. Vernon. He ate with so much relish that he was almost ashamed.

"I have an unusual appetite," he said half apologetically.

"Probably you do not generally dine so late," said Mrs. Vernon.

"No, madam."

"I am glad you enjoy your dinner," said his hostess.

When dinner was over she said, "Come with me into my study, or perhaps I may say my office, and I will give you an idea of your duties."

Robert followed her with not a little curiosity, to a somewhat smaller room on the same floor.

It contained a large writing desk with numerous drawers, also several chairs and a bookcase.

Mrs. Vernon seated herself at the desk.

"Probably you wonder what a woman can want of a secretary?" she said inquiringly.

"No," answered Robert. "I know that there are women of business as well as men."

"Quite true. I do not need to enter into full explanations. However, I may say that I possess considerable property invested in different ways. My husband died two years since, and I am left to manage it for myself."

Robert bowed, indicating that he understood.

"A part of my property is in real estate, and I have numerous tenants. A part is invested in manufacturing stocks. I believe you said you understood bookkeeping?"

"Theoretically, I do. I have studied it in school."

"Take this sheet of paper and write a letter at my dictation."

She rose from the desk and signed to Robert to take her seat.

He did so, and wrote a short letter at her dictation.

"Now give it to me."

She regarded it approvingly.

"That will do very well," she said. "I think you will suit me."

"Am I the first secretary you have employed?" asked Robert curiously.

"A natural question. No, I still have a secretary, a nephew of mine."

Robert looked puzzled.

"Then, with me, you will have two."

"No, for I shall discharge my nephew."

"Is he--a boy?"

"No, he is a young man of twenty-five."

"Do you think I shall suit you any better? I am afraid you will be disappointed in me."

"I will tell you why I discharge my nephew. He takes advantage of his relationship to make suggestions and interfere with my plans. Besides, he is inclined to be gay, and though his duties are by no means arduous he neglects them, and is so careless that I have found numerous errors in his accounts."

"Does he know that he is to be superseded?"

"No; he will learn it first when he sees you."

"I am afraid he will be prejudiced against me."

"No doubt he will."

"Does he depend upon his salary? Won't he be put to inconvenience?"

"You are very considerate. I answer No, for I shall continue to pay him a liberal salary, but will leave him to obtain employment elsewhere. And this leads me to ask your views in regard to compensation."

"I shall be satisfied with whatever you choose to pay me."

"Then suppose we say a hundred dollars a month, and of course a home. You will continue to occupy the room into which Martha conducted you before dinner."

"But, Mrs. Vernon, can I possibly earn as much as that? Most boys of my age are contented with five or six dollars a week."

"They do not have as responsible duties as you. You will not only be my secretary, but will be entrusted with my bank account. I can afford to pay you liberally, and wish to do so."

"Then I can only thank you and accept your generous offer."

"That is well. By the way, how are you provided with money now?"

"I have almost nothing. I have been out of employment for some weeks."

Mrs. Vernon opened a drawer in her desk, and took out a roll of bills.

"Count those, please," she said.

"There are seventy-five dollars."

"You can accept them on account, or rather, I won't charge them to you. You may look upon that sum as your outfit. Very likely you may need to replenish your wardrobe."

"Yes, Mrs. Vernon, I shall, if I am to live in your house."

"Well spoken. As one of my family, of course I shall want you to be well dressed."

"Shall I begin my duties now?"

"No; you may return to your boarding house and prepare to transfer your trunk here."

Robert bowed.

"We shall have supper at seven. Very possibly your predecessor, my nephew, may be here. We will separate till then."

She left the room, and Robert followed.

As he emerged into the street he asked himself whether it were not all a dream. But feeling in his vest pocket he found the roll of bills, and this was a sufficient answer.

What a difference a couple of hours had made in his feelings! In the forenoon he had been discouraged, now he was in the highest spirits.

On his way he passed the furnishing goods store where he had been refused a position in the morning. He was in need of underclothing, and entered.

The proprietor of the shop saw and recognized him.

"You have come back again, I see," he said. "It is of no use. I cannot employ you. So far as I am concerned, I should be willing, but, as you know, my wife is prejudiced against you."

"I am not looking for a position," said Robert quietly.

"What, then?"

"I wish to buy a few articles."

He passed from one article to another, and his bill amounted to over ten dollars.

The proprietor of the store, who waited upon him in person, became more and more amazed, and even a little anxious.

"Can you pay for all these?" he asked.

"Certainly, or I should not buy them."

When the bill was made out it amounted to between fourteen and fifteen dollars. Robert passed out two ten-dollar bills.

"You seem well provided with money," said the merchant respectfully. "Where shall I send these articles?"

Robert gave the number of Mrs. Vernon's residence on Prairie Avenue.

"Do you live there?"

"Yes, sir."

"I hope you will favor me with your continued patronage. Evidently my wife made a very absurd mistake."

Robert did not buy any more articles. He deferred till the next day purchasing a suit, of which he stood in need.

Then it occurred to him, as he had plenty of time, that he would call at the cut-rate ticket office where he had been employed.

As he entered the office he found Livingston Palmer alone.

"I am glad to see you, Robert," said his friend. "I begin to hope that Mr. Gray will take you back."

"How is that?"

"His nephew is getting home-sick. Besides, he has no business in him. He will never make a good clerk. If you can get along for a week or two you may be taken into the office again."

"I am not in the market, Livingston."

"You don't mean to say you have got a place?"

"But I have."

"What is it?"

"I am private secretary to a lady of property on Prairie Avenue."

"You don't say so! Is the pay good?"

"A hundred dollars a month."

"Jumping Jehosophat! You are jollying me."

"Not at all. It's all straight. And that is not all. I have a home in the house, too."

Livingston Palmer regarded his young friend with reverential awe.

"It doesn't seem possible," said he. "How did you get it?"

"I can hardly tell you. The lady has taken me without recommendations."

"Well, Robert, you were born to good luck. I am afraid you won't notice me now that you are getting up in the world."

Robert smiled.

"I will see you as often as I can," he said.

Just then Mr. Gray entered the office.

"Ah, Frost," he said. "I suppose you haven't a place yet?"

"I have one," answered Robert rather coolly, for he felt that the broker had treated him badly.

"Indeed!"

Then after Robert's departure Palmer told his employer the particulars of his late clerk's good fortune. Mr. Gray was disposed to be incredulous.

On returning to Prairie Avenue Robert found himself just in time for tea. At the table he met a stout, swarthy young man, whom Mrs. Vernon introduced as her nephew, Frederic Vernon.

"Is this a new acquaintance of yours, aunt?" asked Frederic Vernon.

"It is my new secretary," she replied, "Robert Frost."

"That boy!" he said disdainfully, regarding Robert with unmistakable animosity.

CHAPTER IV.
THE OLD SECRETARY AND THE NEW.

Before Robert's entrance Frederic Vernon and his aunt had had a conversation. He had no idea that his aunt contemplated a change in their arrangements. She was a woman of a few words, and had been gradually making up her mind to dismiss her nephew from his post as secretary.

When he entered her presence at five o'clock he said apologetically, "I hope you had no important business for me this afternoon, aunt. I was unavoidably detained."

"Please explain, Frederic," she said composedly.

"At the Palmer House I fell in with an old schoolmate who wished me to dine with him."

"And you accepted?"

"Yes; I am awfully sorry."

"Your regrets are unavailing. This is not the first, nor the tenth time, that you have neglected your duties without adequate cause."

Frederic looked at her. She was not in the least excited, but she seemed in earnest.

"I see I shall have to turn over a new leaf," he said to himself. "My aunt is taking it seriously."

"It will be the last time," he said. "I admit that I have been neglectful. Hereafter I will be more attentive."

"It will not be necessary," said Mrs. Vernon.

"Why not?" he asked, in surprise.

"Because I shall relieve you from your duties."

"What do you mean?"

"I shall give you a permanent vacation."

"Do you discharge me?" asked Frederic quickly, his cheek flushing.

"Yes, if you choose to use that word."

"But--how am I to live?"

"I will continue your salary--you may hereafter call it an allowance."

"But how will you manage about your writing?"

"I shall get another secretary--indeed, I have already engaged one."

Frederic Vernon hardly knew how to take this announcement. It was certainly a favorable change for him, as his salary would be continued, and his time would all be at his own disposal.

"I am afraid you are angry with me, aunt?" he said.

"Say dissatisfied."

"But----"

"The fact is, I have thought it best to employ one who was not related to me. You have taken advantage of the relationship to slight my interests. My new secretary is not likely to do that."

"Who is he? Where did you find him?"

"His name is Robert Frost. As to where I found him, I do not consider it necessary to answer that question."

"Is he in the house?"

"He will be here to tea."

Frederic Vernon remained silent for a short time. He was thinking over the new situation. In some respects it was satisfactory. He was naturally lazy, and though his duties had been light, he had no objection to give up work altogether.

"Of course, you will please yourself, aunt," he said.

"There is one thing more. You had better find another home."

"What! Leave this house?"

"Yes; you will be more independent elsewhere. While you were in my service it was best for you to have your home here. I shall make you an extra provision to cover the expense of a room elsewhere."

"You are very kind, aunt."

"I mean to be. Of course, you are at liberty to come here to meals whenever you like. You will be quite independent as regards that."

"How long have you been thinking of making a change, aunt?"

"For some weeks. I advise you to find some occupation. It will not be well for you to have your time entirely unoccupied."

"You are sure this change will not alter your feeling toward me?" he asked anxiously.

"I think not."

Frederic Vernon went upstairs to prepare for tea. Soon after he came down he met Robert, as already mentioned.

He was certainly very much surprised at the youthful appearance of the new secretary, and he was not altogether free from jealousy.

"Have you ever filled the position of secretary before?" he asked abruptly.

"No, Mr. Vernon."

"I supposed not. How old are you?"

"Sixteen."

"Humph! How long since did you lay aside short pants?"

"Frederic!" said his aunt, in a tone of displeasure. "I desire you to drop this tone. I expect you to treat your successor with courtesy. You have nothing to complain of."

"Very well, aunt. I will be guarded by your wishes."

On the whole the young man was not sorry to have his duties transferred to another. Though he had seldom been occupied more than three hours daily, even those had been irksome to him.

"When do you wish me to find a new home, aunt?" he asked.

"You can consult your own convenience."

"I will look around to-morrow, then. Do you wish me to initiate my successor in the duties of his position?"

"It will not be necessary. They are simple, and I will give him all the aid he requires."

When they rose from the table Frederic Vernon invited Robert to go out with him.

"I will take you to some place of amusement," he said.

His object was to get better acquainted with his successor, and report unfavorably to his aunt.

"Thank you," answered Robert. "You are very kind, but I am tired, and I should like to arrange my clothing in my chamber. Some other time I shall be glad to accept your invitation."

"Very well," said Vernon indifferently, and soon left.

"I am glad you did not go out with my nephew," said Mrs. Vernon. "He keeps late hours, which would be even worse for a boy of your age than for him."

"I am afraid he is not pleased with my taking his place."

"Probably not; though he won't object to being relieved from all care. Perhaps I had better tell you something about our relations. He is a son of an older brother of my husband, and should I die without a will, he is my natural heir. I fancy he bears this in mind, and that it prevents his making any exertions in his own behalf. I don't mind confessing that I am a rich woman, and that my property would be well worth inheriting."

"Still," said Robert, "you are likely to live a good many years."

"Perhaps so, but I am twenty years older than my nephew. He is a young man of fair abilities, and might achieve a creditable success in business if he were not looking forward to my fortune."

Mrs. Vernon seemed quite confidential, considering their brief acquaintance.

"At any rate," said Robert, smiling, "I hope I am not likely to be spoiled by any such anticipation."

"Some time you shall tell me of your family. Now it may be well to go up to your room and arrange your things."

Robert went upstairs, and retired early, feeling fatigued. He could not help congratulating himself on the favorable change in his circumstances. In the morning he had been despondent and almost penniless. Now he felt almost rich.

The next morning after breakfast Mrs. Vernon said: "Be ready to go downtown with me at two o'clock. I will introduce you at my bank, as I shall have occasion to send you there at times to draw and deposit money."

"When shall you wish me to write for you, Mrs. Vernon?"

"To-day, just after dinner. It will not always be at the same hour."

They set out at the time mentioned. Mrs. Vernon introduced Robert to the teller at what we will call the Bank of Chicago, and announced that he would act as her messenger and agent.

As they left the bank she said: "I shall now leave you to your own devices--only stipulating that you be at home at two o'clock."

"It seems I am to have an easy time," thought Robert, when left alone.

In one of the cross streets leading from Clark to State Street Robert met Frederic Vernon and a friend.

"Hallo, Frost!" said the former. "Have you been out with my aunt?"

"Yes, sir."

"Cameron, this is Mr. Frost, my aunt's private secretary."

"I thought you filled that honorable position," said Cameron.

"So I did, but I have resigned it--that is, the place, but not the salary."

"You are in luck. Won't your friend come in with us and have a drink?"

"Thank you for the invitation," said Robert, "but I must ask you to excuse me."

"Oh, you are Puritanical," said Cameron, with an unpleasant sneer.

"Perhaps so."

Robert bowed and passed on.

"Do you know, Vernon," said Cameron, "I have seen that kid before, and under peculiar circumstances."

"Indeed!"

"Yes; on Tuesday I was in the Bazaar dry goods store, on State Street, when I saw him for the first time."

"What were the peculiar circumstances?"

"He was charged with stealing a pocket-book."

"Are you sure of that?" asked Vernon eagerly.

"Yes, I should know him anywhere."

"How did he get off?"

"Some minister spoke in his favor."

"I must tell my aunt of this," said Vernon gleefully. "I think the young man will get his walking papers."

CHAPTER V.
A PLOT AGAINST ROBERT.

Frederic Vernon lost no time in acquainting his aunt with his discovery.

Finding himself alone with her that evening, he said: "I am afraid, aunt, you did not exercise much caution when you selected young Frost as your secretary."

"Explain yourself, Frederic."

"It is only a few days since he was arrested for theft in a dry goods store."

"Well?"

"Surely you don't approve of employing a thief?"

"No, but he was innocent."

"How do you know? Does he say so?"

"I was in the store when he was arrested."

"And yet you engaged him?"

"The arrest was a mistake. The real thief was found and is now serving a sentence."

"I didn't suppose you knew of this incident in the life of your secretary."

"And you hoped to injure him by mentioning it to me."

"I thought you would see that you had made a bad choice."

"Then you made a mistake. Thus far I am quite satisfied with my choice."

Frederic Vernon was mortified by his lack of success, but determined to follow up his attack upon Robert, and to get him into trouble if he could. He had still free entrance into the house of his aunt, and occasionally occupied his own room there.

One day in passing his aunt's chamber, seeing the door ajar, he entered, and soon discovered on her bureau a valuable ring.

"Ha!" he exclaimed, as a contemptible thought entered his mind. "I think I can give young Frost some trouble."

He took the ring, and carrying it into Robert's room, put it in a drawer of the bureau. In the evening he took supper in the house. His aunt looked perplexed.

"What is the matter, aunt?" he asked.

"I miss my diamond ring--the cluster diamond--which was a gift from your uncle."

"That is serious. When did you see it last?"

"I think I left it on my bureau this morning. Of course, it was careless, but I felt that there was no danger of its being lost or taken."

"Humph! I don't know about that. Was it valuable?"

"I suppose so. In fact, a jeweler told me once that it was worth five hundred dollars."

"It might tempt a thief. Aunt, let me make a suggestion."

"Well?"

"I slept here last night. I should like to have you search my chamber to make sure it is not there."

"Nonsense, Frederic! As if I could suspect you."

"No, it is not nonsense. What do you say, Mr. Frost?"

"I am perfectly willing to have my room searched, Mr. Vernon."

"I don't suspect either of you," said Mrs. Vernon. "I will look again in my own room."

"Aunt, that will be well, but I insist on your searching my room also, and Mr. Frost is willing to have you search his."

Reluctantly Mrs. Vernon followed her nephew upstairs, and first examined her own chamber, but the ring was not found.

Next she entered Frederic's room. He made great ado of opening all the drawers of his bureau, and searching every available place, but again the ring was not found.

"You see, the search is unnecessary, Frederic," said his aunt.

"Still I shall feel better for its having been made."

"Then we will stop here."

"If Robert does not want his room searched he can say so," said Vernon significantly.

Robert colored, for he felt the insinuation.

"I wish you to search my room," he said proudly.

Frederic Vernon conducted the examination.

He searched every other place first. Finally he opened a small drawer of the bureau, and uttered an exclamation.

"What is this?" he asked, as he drew out the ring and held it up. "Is this your ring, aunt?"

"Yes," she answered calmly.

"Mrs. Vernon," said Robert, in an agitated tone, "I hope you don't think I had anything to do with taking the ring."

"The case is plain," said Frederic Vernon severely. "You may as well confess, and I will ask my aunt to let you off. Of course she cannot retain you in her employ, but I will ask her not to prosecute you."

Robert looked anxiously yet proudly into the face of his employer.

"Don't feel anxious, Robert," she said, "I haven't the slightest suspicion of you."

"Then, aunt, how do you account for the ring being found in the room of your secretary?"

"Because," said Mrs. Vernon, "it was placed there."

"Exactly. That is my opinion."

"But not by him."

"Not by him? What do you mean?"

"By you. I was in my room this afternoon, and heard steps in his chamber; I knew that it was not Robert, for I had sent him out on an errand. Presently you came downstairs. It was you who placed the ring where it was found, Frederic Vernon," she said sternly.

"If that is the opinion you have of me, aunt," said Vernon, who could not help betraying confusion, "I will bid you good-evening."

"You may as well. Your attempt to ruin the reputation of your successor by a false charge is contemptible."

Vernon did not attempt to answer this accusation, but turning on his heel left the room.

"Thank you for your justice, Mrs. Vernon," said Robert gratefully. "I was afraid you might believe me a thief."

"I should not, even if I had not positive knowledge that Frederic had entered into a conspiracy against you. He has done himself no good by this base attempt to blacken your reputation. We will let the matter drop and think no more of it."

CHAPTER VI.
MRS. VERNON'S MONEY.

During the next three months Frederic Vernon was a rare visitor at the house of his aunt. He took apartments nearer the central part of the city, and lived like a bachelor of large means. The result was, that he overrun the income received from his aunt, though this was a very liberal one.

He applied to her to increase his allowance, but she firmly refused.

"How is it, Frederic," she asked, "that you are spending so much money?"

"I don't know, aunt. I only know that the money goes."

"You must be a very poor manager."

"I have a good many friends--from the best families in Chicago."

"And I suppose you entertain them frequently?"

"It is expected of me."

"I give you twice as much as you received when you were my secretary."

"Then I did not have an establishment of my own."

"You ought to live well on three thousand dollars a year."

"Do you live on that, aunt?"

"I keep up a large house."

"And I have an extensive suite of rooms."

"It is not necessary. What rent do you pay?"

"A thousand dollars a year."

"Then you will need to engage cheaper rooms."

"Won't you help me out, aunt?"

"No," answered Mrs. Vernon firmly.

Frederic went away in ill humor.

He was never rude to Robert now. Indeed, he treated him with exaggerated and formal respect, which Robert felt only veiled a feeling of dislike.

One evening Robert sat down for a time in the lobby of a prominent hotel. He did not at first notice that Frederic Vernon and a tall black-whiskered man of middle age sat near him, conversing in a low tone. At length he heard something that startled him.

"Is it difficult," asked Frederic, "to procure the seclusion of a party who shows plain signs of insanity? I ask you as a physician."

"State your case," said his companion.

"I have an aunt," answered Frederic, "a woman of fifty or more, who is acting in a very eccentric manner."

"In what way?"

"Until a few months since she employed me as her private secretary. Without any warning and with no excuse for the action, she discharged me, and engaged in my place a boy of sixteen, whom she had known only a day or two."

"Where did she meet this boy?"

"In a large dry goods store, under peculiar circumstances. He was about to be arrested for theft when she secured his release, and engaged him as her secretary on a liberal salary."

"Is he still in her employ?"

"Yes. She has made him her first favorite, and it looks very much as if she intended to make him her heir."

"Is she a rich woman?"

"She is probably worth quarter of a million--perhaps more."

"And you are her rightful heir?"

"Yes. What do you think of that?"

"It is very hard on you."

"Don't you think it is evidence of insanity?"

"It looks very much that way."

"If you can manage to procure her confinement in an asylum, I will make it worth your while, and can afford to do so. I should in that case, doubtless, have the custody of her property, and----"

Robert did not hear the balance of the sentence, for the two parties arose and left the hotel, leaving him startled and shocked by the revelations of the wicked conspiracy which so seriously threatened the safety of his benefactress.

He lost no time in giving Mrs. Vernon information of what he had heard.

"You are quite sure of what you have told me?" she asked, with deep interest.

"Certainly, Mrs. Vernon. Why do you ask?"

"Because it seemed to me incredible that Frederic could be guilty of such base ingratitude. Why, he is even now in receipt of an income of three thousand dollars a year from me."

"It seems very ungrateful."

"It is very ungrateful," said the widow in an emphatic tone.

"Mrs. Vernon," said Robert, "your nephew mentioned as one evidence of your insanity your employing me as your secretary. If this is going to expose you to danger, perhaps you had better discharge me."

"Give me your hand, Robert," said Mrs. Vernon impulsively. "It is easy to see that you are a true friend, though in no way related to me."

"I hope to prove so."

"And you would really be willing that I should discharge you and take back my nephew into his old place?"

"Yes."

"Nothing would induce me to do it. That ungrateful young man I will never receive into a confidential and trusted position. What is the appearance of the man you saw with him?"

Robert described him.

"You think he was a physician?"

"I judge so."

"Probably my nephew will bring him here to see me with a view to reporting against my sanity. In that case I shall call upon you to identify him," concluded Mrs. Vernon.

CHAPTER VII.
THE DOCTOR'S VISIT.

Two days later Frederic Vernon called. He found his aunt with Robert. The latter was writing to her dictation.

"Are you well, aunt?" he asked blithely.

"Yes, Frederic. This is an unusual time for you to call. Have you any special business with me?"

"Oh, no, aunt, but I happened to be passing. I have a friend with me. Will you allow me to introduce him?"

"Yes."

"Then I will go down and bring him up. I left him in the hall."

When her nephew left the room Mrs. Vernon said rapidly, "Stay here, Robert, when my nephew comes back. If the man with him is the same one you saw at the hotel make me a signal."

"Yes, Mrs. Vernon."

Frederic Vernon entered with his companion.

"Aunt," he said, "let me introduce my friend Mr. Remington. Remington, my aunt, Mrs. Vernon."

Mrs. Vernon bowed formally, and did not seem to see the outstretched hand of her nephew's companion. She scrutinized him carefully, however.

"Are you a business man, Mr. Remington?" she asked.

"No, madam," answered Remington hesitatingly.

"Professional then?"

"My friend Remington is a physician," said Frederic. "I should have introduced him as Dr. Remington."

"Perhaps you are a patient of his?"

"Oh, no," laughed Frederic. "I don't need any medical services."

"Nor I," said Mrs. Vernon quickly.

"By the way," said Frederic, turning toward Robert, "this is Mr. Frost, my aunt's private secretary."

Dr. Remington surveyed our hero closely.

"He is young for so important a position," he said.

"Yes, he is young, but competent and reliable," answered Mrs. Vernon.

"No doubt, no doubt! Probably you have known him for a long time, and felt justified in engaging him, though so young."

"Certainly I felt justified," said Mrs. Vernon haughtily.

"Oh, of course, of course."

The conversation continued for a few minutes, Mrs. Vernon limiting herself for the most part to answering questions asked by her nephew. She treated the stranger with distant coldness.

Presently Frederic Vernon arose.

"We mustn't stay any longer, Remington," he said. "We interrupted my aunt, and must not take up too much of her time."

"You are right," said the doctor. "Mrs. Vernon, I am very glad to have made your acquaintance."

Mrs. Vernon bowed politely, but did not otherwise acknowledge the compliment.

"Good-by, aunt," said Frederic lightly. "I will call again soon."

"When you find time," she answered coldly.

"Good-by, Robert," said Frederic, in an affable tone.

Robert bowed.

"Well, Remington," said Frederic when they emerged into the street. "What do you say?"

"I say that your aunt treated us both with scant courtesy."

"She reserves that for young Frost, her secretary. He is first favorite, and is working to make himself her heir."

"We will put a spoke in his wheel," said the physician. "I shall have no hesitation in giving you a certificate of your aunt's probable insanity."

"Good! I will see that you are properly compensated."

"That sounds very well, Frederic, but is too indefinite."

"What do you want, then?"

"If through my means your aunt is adjudged insane, and you come into her fortune, or get control of her estate, I want ten thousand dollars."

"Isn't that rather steep?"

"You say Mrs. Vernon is worth at least quarter of a million?"

"I judge so."

"Then what I ask is little enough. You must remember that I must get another doctor to sign with me."

"Very well, I agree," answered Vernon after a pause.

"Then I will undertake it. Be guided by me, and success is sure."

When the pair of conspirators had left her presence Mrs. Vernon remained for a short time silent and thoughtful. Robert watched her anxiously.

"I hope," he said, "you do not think there is cause for alarm."

"I do not know," she answered. "I am not so much alarmed as disgusted. That my own nephew should enter into such a plot is enough to destroy one's confidence in human nature."

"If my going away would lessen the danger----"

"No; I shall need you more than ever. I am not prepared to say just yet what I shall do, but I shall soon decide. We will stop work for this afternoon. I am going downtown to see my lawyer. I shall not need you till tea-time."

She left the room, and Robert, availing himself of his leisure, left the house also.

He was destined to a surprise.

On State Street, near the Palmer House, an hour later he came face to face with his step-father, now in the city for the first time since his illness. Robert had held no communication with the family since obtaining his new position, and James Talbot did not know where he was.

"Robert Frost!" he exclaimed in genuine surprise.

"Mr. Talbot," said Robert coldly.

"Are you still living in Chicago?" asked his step-father curiously.

"Yes, sir. Is my mother well?"

"As well as she can be, considering the waywardness of her son."

"What do you mean by that?" demanded Robert with spirit. "My only waywardness consists in resenting your interference with my liberty."

"I was only exercising my right as your step-father."

"My mother's act has made you my step-father, but I don't admit that it gives you the right to order me about."

"It is very sad to see you so headstrong," said James Talbot, in a mournful tone.

"Don't trouble yourself about me, Mr. Talbot. I feel competent to regulate my own affairs."

"I suppose you are working in some way?" said Talbot inquiringly.

"Yes, sir."

"I heard you had left Gray's office. For whom are you working? Are you in a store?"

"No, sir."

"You seem well-dressed. I hope you are doing well?"

"Yes."

"Have you any message for your mother?"

"Tell her I will write to her again soon. I ought to have done so before."

"You had better go home with me; I invite you to do so."

"I do not care to be under the same roof with you."

"It is sad, indeed, to see a boy of your age so refractory."

"Don't borrow any trouble on my account, Mr. Talbot. I will go home on one condition."

"What is that?"

"That you will leave the house."

"This is very improper and disrespectful. Of course I cannot do that. I shall remain to comfort and care for your mother."

"Then there is no more to say. Good-day, sir."

Robert bowed slightly, and passed on.

"I wish I knew what he was doing, and where he is employed," said Talbot to himself. "I would let his employer know how he has behaved to me. I wish he might lose his place and be compelled to sue for pardon."

When Robert met Mrs. Vernon at the supper table she said to him, "Robert, I have some news for you."

"What is it, Mrs. Vernon?"

"We start for New York to-morrow. We sail for Liverpool on Saturday."

CHAPTER VIII.
FREDERIC VERNON'S PERPLEXITY.

There are few boys to whom the prospect of visiting Europe would not possess a charm. Robert was delighted by Mrs. Vernon's announcement, and readily agreed to assist her in the necessary preparations. Nothing occurred to interfere with their plans. They passed a single day in New York, where Mrs. Vernon purchased a large letter of credit, and Saturday saw their departure on a Cunard steamer bound for Liverpool.

It was on this very day that Frederic Vernon, again accompanied by his friend, Dr. Remington, called at the house on Prairie Avenue. The doctor recommended a second interview, in order that he might more plausibly give a certificate of insanity. No hint of Mrs. Vernon's projected trip had reached her treacherous nephew. A single servant had been placed in charge by Mrs. Vernon to care for the house, and guard against the intrusion of burglars.

"I suppose my aunt is at home, Martha," said Frederic blithely.

"No, Mr. Frederic, she has gone away."

"You mean she has gone into the city. When will she return?"

"I don't know."

"Why don't you know?"

"She has gone on a journey."

"Indeed!" said Remington, much disappointed. "Where has she gone?"

"She said she might go to California."

Martha had been instructed to say this, and did not know but it was true.

"Well, well! That is strange!" ejaculated Remington.

"What do you think of it, doctor?"

"It bears out our theory," responded the doctor briefly.

"It is very inconvenient," Vernon continued. "When did Mrs. Vernon start?" he inquired, turning to the girl.

"On Wednesday morning."

Remington's countenance fell.

"I suppose it will be of no use to remain longer, then," he said, as he descended the steps. "Is there no one of whom you can obtain information, Vernon?"

"My aunt has a man of business who looks after her investments. He will probably know."

"Let us go there, then."

Mr. Farley's office was on Dearborn Street. Frederic Vernon went there at once. Mr. Farley was a lawyer as well as a man of business, and Frederic had to wait half an hour while he was occupied with a client.

"Well, Mr. Vernon, what can I do for you?" he asked coldly, for the young man was not a favorite of his.

"I just called upon my aunt, and learned that she had departed on a journey."

"Precisely so."

"The servant thought she had gone to California. Is that correct?"

"Did she not write to inform you of her destination?"

"No, sir, she was probably too hurried. Of course you know where she is."

"Even if I did know I should not be at liberty to tell you. If your aunt has not informed you, she probably has her reasons."

Vernon flushed, and he found it hard to control his anger.

"Then you refuse to tell me?"

"I do not feel called upon to tell. Have you any special business with your aunt? If so, I will mention it in any letter I may have occasion to write."

"It seems to me this is a very foolish mystery."

"It is not for me, or for you, to comment upon or to criticise your aunt's plans," said the lawyer pointedly.

"Has Robert Frost, whom she employs as secretary, gone with her?"

"Possibly. She did not mention him in her last interview with me."

"Will you write me when you hear from her?"

"If she authorizes it."

"I will leave you my address."

There seemed to be nothing more to say, and Vernon left the office baffled and perplexed. He communicated what he had heard to Dr. Remington, whom he had not thought it advisable to take with him to Mr. Farley's office.

"What do you make of it, Remington?" he inquired.

"I don't know. Do you think Mrs. Vernon got any inkling of your scheme to have her adjudged insane?"

"How could she?"

"True. We have been very careful not to discuss the matter within the hearing of anyone."

"What can we do?"

"We must wait. You must find out where your aunt is before you can take any steps."

"Suppose she has gone to California?"

"We can follow her."

There was, however, one serious impediment in the way of going to California. Vernon used up his allowance as fast as he received it, and was even a little in debt. Again, California was a large place, and though probably his aunt might be in San Francisco, it was by no means certain. The money, however, was the chief consideration.

"How are you fixed financially, Remington?" asked Vernon.

"Why do you ask?"

"If you could lend me five hundred dollars we might start tomorrow."

"Where do you think I could raise five hundred dollars?" asked Remington coolly.

"I thought you might have it--in a savings bank."

"I wish I had, but even then I should consider it safer there than in your hands."

"I hope you don't doubt my honesty," said Vernon quickly.

"Well, I haven't the money, so there is no occasion to say more on the subject."

Vernon looked despondent.

"What do you advise me to do?" he asked.

"When does your next allowance come due?"

"On the first of next month."

"Three weeks hence?"

"Yes."

"Then you will have to wait till that time, unless you find some obliging friend who has more money than I."

"It's very vexatious."

"It may be for our advantage. Remember, it is not at all certain that your aunt is in California. You may get some light on the subject within a short time. Next week suppose you call in Prairie Avenue again. The servant may have heard something."

"True," responded Vernon, somewhat encouraged.

In a few days he called again, but Martha had heard nothing.

"It is hardly time yet," said Remington. "Next week you may have better luck. If your aunt is in California there would be time for her to get settled and write to you."

The next week Vernon ascended the steps of his aunt's house with a degree of confidence.

"I think I shall get some information this time," he said.

"Have you had a letter from my aunt yet?" he asked.

"No, Mr. Frederic."

His countenance fell.

"But I have received a note from Mr. Farley."

"What did he say?" asked Vernon eagerly.

"He said that he had had a telegram from my mistress and she was well."

"Did he say where she was?"

"No, sir."

"And you have no idea?"

"No, Mr. Frederic. I expect she is in California, as I told you."

"But why should she telegraph from California?"

This question was asked of his companion.

"I give it up," said Remington. "You might call on Farley again."

"I will."

The visit, however, yielded no satisfaction. The lawyer admitted that he had received a telegram. He positively refused to account for its being a telegram, and not a letter.

"But," said Vernon, "do you feel justified in keeping me ignorant of the whereabouts of my near relative?"

"Yes, since she has not thought it necessary to inform you."

"By the way, Mr. Farley," asked Vernon, after a pause, "can you kindly advance me a part of my next month's allowance?"

"It will all be payable within a week."

"True, but I have occasion for a little money. Fifty dollars will do."

"You must excuse me, Mr. Vernon."

As Frederic Vernon's available funds were reduced to twenty-five cents, this refusal was embarrassing. However, he succeeded in borrowing fifty dollars during the day from a broker who knew his circumstances, at five per cent. a month, giving the broker an order on Mr. Farley dated a week later.

The same evening found him in the billiard room of the Palmer House, playing a game of billiards with Remington.

Remington took up a copy of the New York Herald, and glanced over the columns in a desultory way. Something caught his eye, and he exclaimed in an excited tone, "Vernon, the mystery is solved. Your aunt is at the Charing Cross Hotel in London."

"You don't mean it?" ejaculated Vernon.

"See for yourself. Mrs. Ralph Vernon, Chicago; Robert Frost, Chicago."

Frederic Vernon gazed at his friend in stupefaction.

"I can't believe it," he muttered feebly.

CHAPTER IX.
ROBERT REACHES LONDON.

The ocean trip was more enjoyed by Robert than by Mrs. Vernon. For three days the lady was quite seasick, while her young secretary was not at all affected. He was indefatigable in his attentions to the invalid, and gained a stronger hold upon her affections.

"I don't know what I should do without you, Robert," she said on the third day. "You seem to me almost like a son."

"I am glad to hear you say this, Mrs. Vernon," returned Robert, adding with a smile, "if you had said I seemed to you almost like a nephew, I should not have been so well pleased."

"I should like to forget that I have a nephew," said Mrs. Vernon, with momentary bitterness. "I shall never forget his treachery and ingratitude."

Robert did not follow up the subject. Frederic Vernon's ingratitude to his aunt and benefactress seemed to him thoroughly base, but he did not care to prejudice Mrs. Vernon against him.

"I wish you were my nephew," continued Mrs. Vernon thoughtfully. "I cannot help contrasting your treatment of me to his."

"I have reason to be grateful to you," said Robert. "I was very badly situated when you took me in."

"I feel repaid for all I have done for you, Robert," said Mrs. Vernon. "But now go on deck and enjoy the bright sunshine and the glorious breeze."

"I wish you could go with me."

"So do I. I think I shall be able to accompany you to-morrow."

Mrs. Vernon felt so much better the next day that she was able to spend a part of the time on deck, and from that time a portion of every day was devoted to out-of-door exercise. She was able to walk on deck supported by Robert, who was never so occupied with the new friends he made among the passengers as to make him neglectful of his benefactress.

Mrs. Vernon, too, made some acquaintances.

"How devoted your son is to you, Mrs. Vernon," said Mrs. Hathaway, an elderly widow from the city of New York. "I wish I had a son, but alas! I am childless."

"So am I," said Mrs. Vernon quietly.

Mrs. Hathaway looked surprised.

"Is he not your son, then?"

"He is not related to me in any way."

"I am surprised to hear it. What then is the secret of your companionship?"

"He is my private secretary."

"And he so young! Is he competent to serve you in that capacity?"

"Entirely so. He is thoroughly well educated and entirely reliable."

"If you ever feel disposed to part with him, transfer him to me."

Mrs. Vernon smiled.

"Have you no near relatives, then?"

"No, I once had a son, who died about the age of your young secretary. I should be glad if you would transfer him to me. I am rich, and I would see that he was well provided for."

"I don't think I could spare him. I too am rich, and I can provide for him."

"If you change your mind my offer holds good."

Later in the day when they were together Mrs. Vernon said, "Robert, I don't know but I ought to increase your salary."

"You pay me more now than anyone else would."

"I am not sure of that. I have had an application to transfer you to another party."

"Any person on this steamer?"

"Yes; Mrs. Hathaway."

"Does she need a private secretary?"

"Probably not, but she says you are about the age of a son she lost. I think she wants you to supply his place. She is rich, and might do more for you than I am doing."

"I am quite satisfied with my present position. I do not want to leave you."

Mrs. Vernon looked gratified.

"I do not want to lose you," she said, "but I thought it only fair to speak of Mrs. Hathaway's offer."

"I am very much obliged to her, but I prefer to remain with you."

Mrs. Vernon looked pleased.

"I should be willing to transfer my nephew Frederic to Mrs. Hathaway," she said, "but I doubt if the arrangement would prove satisfactory to her."

The voyage was a brief one, their steamer being one of the swiftest of the Cunard liners, and a week had scarcely passed when they reached the pier at Liverpool. A short stay in Liverpool, and they took the train for London, where they took rooms at the Charing Cross Hotel. Robert was excited and pleased with what he saw of the great metropolis. He had his forenoon to himself. Mrs. Vernon had visited London fifteen years before, and had seen the principal objects of interest in the city. She rose late, and did not require Robert's presence till one o'clock.

"Go about freely," she said. "You will want to see the Tower, and Westminster Abbey, and the Houses of Parliament. I don't care to see them a second time."

"But I don't feel quite right in leaving you."

"Don't feel any solicitude for me. I am three times your age, and our tastes and interests naturally differ. When I need you, I shall signify it, but it will seldom be till afternoon."

In the afternoon they often took a carriage and drove in the parks or out into the country. So between the drives and his own explorations Robert was in a fair way of becoming well acquainted with the great metropolitan district.

One afternoon, about a week after their arrival, Mrs. Vernon said with a smile: "To-morrow morning I shall require your presence."

"Certainly, Mrs. Vernon."

"We will go out at eleven o'clock. It is on business of your own."

"Business of my own?" repeated Robert, wondering what it would be. "I will be ready."

At eleven o'clock Robert ordered a hansom cab, and the driver awaited directions.

"Do you know the office of Baring Brothers, bankers?" asked Mrs. Vernon.

"Yes, madam."

"Take us there."

It was on the firm of Baring Brothers that Mrs. Vernon had a letter of credit, and Robert concluded that she was intending to draw some money from them. He did not connect her errand with himself.

Arrived at the banking house, Robert remained in an outer room, while Mrs. Vernon was closeted with a member of the firm.

After twenty minutes Robert was called in.

"Robert," said Mrs. Vernon, "you will append your signature here."

"Then this is the young gentleman for whom you have established a credit with us?" said the banker.

"Yes, sir."

"He is very young."

"Sixteen years old."

"Do you wish him to have a guardian?"

"No. He is to have absolute control of the funds in your charge."

When they emerged from the banking house Mrs. Vernon said: "Robert, I will explain what probably mystifies you. I have placed to your credit with Baring Brothers the sum of four hundred pounds. It is at your own control."

Robert looked inexpressibly astonished. He knew that four hundred pounds represented about two thousand dollars in American money.

"What have I done to deserve such liberality?" he asked gratefully.

"You have become the friend that my nephew ought to have been. I am rich, as you are probably aware, and shall be unable to carry my money with me when I die. I might, of course, make a will, and leave you the sum I have now given, but the will would probably be contested by my nephew if he should survive me, and I have determined to prevent that by giving you the money in my lifetime. How far Frederic Vernon will be my heir I cannot as yet tell. It will depend to a considerable extent upon his conduct. Whatever happens, I shall have the satisfaction of feeling that I have shown my appreciation of your loyalty and fidelity."

"I don't know what to say, Mrs. Vernon. I hope you will believe that I am grateful," answered Robert warmly.

"I am sure of it. I have every confidence in you, Robert."

To Robert the events of the morning seemed like a wonderful dream. Three months before he had been wandering about the streets of Chicago a poor boy in search of employment. Now he was worth two thousand dollars, in receipt of a large income, and able to lay by fifty dollars a month. But above all, he was made independent of his step-father, whose attempts to control him were more than ever futile. This led him to think that he ought to apprise his mother of his present whereabouts and his health. He did not think it advisable to mention the large gift he had just received, or the amount of the salary he was receiving, though he had no doubt it would change the feelings of Mr. Talbot toward him. His step-father worshiped success, and if he knew that Robert was so well provided for he would do all that lay in his power to ingratiate himself with him.

After writing the letter to his mother, he wrote as follows to his fellow-clerk, Livingston Palmer, whom he had not informed of his European journey.

> "Dear Friend Palmer," he wrote, "you will be surprised to hear that I am in London, and shall probably spend several months on this side of the water. I am still acting as private secretary to Mrs. Vernon, who continues to be kind and liberal. From time to time I will write to you. I inclose a ten-dollar bill as a present, and shall be glad to have you spend it in any way that is agreeable to yourself.
>
> "Yours sincerely,
> "Robert Frost."

CHAPTER X.
MATTERS AT HOME.

James Talbot was thoroughly put out by the way in which Robert had treated him when the two had met on the street in Chicago.

"That boy hasn't the least respect for me," was what he told himself bitterly. "I am afraid he will end up by making me a lot of trouble."

Before his sickness he had felt certain that he would get at least ten thousand dollars of the Frost fortune in his hands,--to be invested, so he had told Mrs. Talbot, in the real estate business in Chicago. What he was really going to do with the cash, the man had not yet decided. Certain it is, however, that neither Mrs. Talbot nor Robert would have ever seen a dollar of it again.

When James Talbot arrived home he was so out of humor that even his wife noticed it.

"You are not well again," she said.

"I met that boy of yours," he growled.

"You met Robert!" she exclaimed. "Where?"

"On the street, in Chicago."

"How was he looking?"

"Oh, he was well enough, madam. But let me tell you, that boy is going to the dogs."

"Oh, I trust not, James."

"I say he is."

"Did you two quarrel?"

"He quarreled; I did not. I invited him to come back home, and what do you think he said?"

"I cannot say."

"Said he wouldn't come back unless I got out. Said that to me, his legal step-father," stormed Talbot.

"I am very sorry you and Robert cannot get along," sighed the lady meekly.

"It's the boy's fault. He is a--a terror. He will end up in prison, mark my words."

"I do not think so," answered Mrs. Talbot, and to avoid a scene she quitted the room.

James Talbot was growing desperate, since the little money he had had of his own was nearly all spent. By hook or by crook he felt that he must get something out of his wife.

A few days later he concocted a scheme to further his own interests. Coming home from the post-office, he rushed into his wife's presence with a face full of smiles.

"Sarah, I have struck a bonanza!" he cried, waving a folded legal-looking document over his head.

"A bonanza?" she queried, looking up from her sewing in wonder.

"Yes, a bonanza. I have the chance to make half a million dollars."

"In what way?"

"By investing in a dock property in Chicago, on the river. My friend, Millet, put me on to the deal. The property is to be sold at private sale, and Millet and I are going to buy it in--that is, if we can raise the necessary cash."

"Is it so valuable?"

"We can get the property for twenty-five thousand dollars. It is right next to the docks of the Dearborn Iron Manufacturing Company. They wanted this land, but the owner quarreled with them and wouldn't let them have it. Now we can gather it in for about half its value, and it won't be a year before the iron people will offer us a fat sum for it."

"But if the iron people want it, why don't they get a private party to buy it in for them?" returned Mrs. Talbot.

"Oh, you women don't understand these things," answered James Talbot loftily. "Millet has the bargain clinched--if only we can raise the money."

"And how much will he raise?"

"Twelve thousand dollars. He wants me to put in the other thirteen thousand. My dear, you will lend me that amount, won't you? It would be a crime to let such a chance slip by."

"Don't you know that thirteen is an unlucky number?" said the lady slowly.

"Surely, Sarah, you are not as superstitious as all that. If you are, I'll get Millet to put up even with me--twelve thousand and five hundred each. But I would rather have the balance of the say in the matter."

"I am not superstitious, James, but--but----"

"But what? The money will be perfectly safe."

"I--I think I had better have a lawyer look into the deal first. There may be some flaw in the title to the property."

"No, that is all right--Millet had it examined. There is no time to spare, as the deal must be closed by noon to-morrow, or our option comes to an end."

"It is very sudden."

"And that is how fortunes are made, my love. The man of business watches his chances, and then seizes them before anybody else can get ahead of him."

Mrs. Talbot was doubtful, and tried to argue. But her husband seemed so positive that he at last won her over, and got her to make out a check for the thirteen thousand dollars.

"But be careful, James," she pleaded. "Remember, I do not consider this money really mine. At my death it must go to Robert."

"I shall be careful, Sarah, my love," he said. "Do not worry."

But to himself he thought: "That boy, always that boy! It will be a long day before he sets eyes on a cent of this money!"

He could hardly control his delight, but he did his best to calm his feelings before his wife.

The next day he was off for Chicago, stating that he would not be back again for several days.

Secretly, Mrs. Talbot was much worried over what she had done.

"I hope the investment proves a good one," she thought. "I would not wish to see the money lost. It must all go to Robert when I am gone." She never considered that the Frost fortune was her own, for hers was, as we know, only a life interest.

Two days later came a letter from Robert--not the one mailed from London, but one he had penned in New York before taking the trip on the ocean liner.

Mrs. Talbot was greatly interested in all her son had to say. She was glad he was enjoying good health, and pleased to know that he would write again on reaching the other side of the Atlantic.

On the same day that she received Robert's letter a visitor called upon her. It was William Frankwell, her lawyer, and a man who had at one time transacted all of Mr. Frost's legal business for him.

"You will excuse me for calling, Mrs. Talbot," said the lawyer, after the usual greeting. "But I thought it might be for your interest to drop in."

"I am glad to see you, Mr. Frankwell," she responded. "I was thinking of sending for you."

"Indeed. Was it about that check?"

"What do you know of the check?" she cried.

"I heard of it at the bank, and I thought----"

The lawyer paused.

"That it was rather unusual for me to put out a check of that size?"

"Exactly."

"Mr. Talbot is going to use it in buying a dock property in Chicago."

And she gave the lawyer what particulars she possessed regarding the transaction.

"If things are as you say, they are all right," said the lawyer.

"Mr. Frankwell, I wish you to look into the matter, and--and----"

"And see if everything is as represented," he finished.

"Yes. I am ashamed to own it, but my husband is--well, is not exactly what I took him to be," she faltered.

"I understand, perfectly, Mrs. Talbot," answered William Frankwell gravely. "I will do my best for you."

"I should not wish him to know that I am having an investigation made."

"He shall not know it--I give you my word on that."

And so they parted, and the lawyer set one of his clerks to watching James Talbot, to learn just what the man's underhanded work meant.

CHAPTER XI.
VERNON MAKES ANOTHER MOVE.

Frederic Vernon was much put out to think that his aunt had gone to England instead of to California.

"What do you think of this?" he asked of Dr. Remington.

"I think your aunt wanted to put you off the track," replied the physician.

"That she had no idea of going to California, even at first?"

"That's it."

"Do you think she suspects what we intend to do?"

"Perhaps," was the dry reply. "Insane people are quite crafty, you know."

"Oh, she must be insane, Remington."

"Well, I am willing to give a certificate to that effect, and I can get another doctor to back me up."

"But we can't touch her in England, can we?"

"I think not. You must try some means of getting her back to the United States."

"That is easy enough to say, but not so easy to do," returned Frederic Vernon gloomily.

"Make it necessary for her to return."

"How can I?"

"Do you know how her capital is invested?"

"In various investments,--banks, stocks, and bonds, besides some real estate."

"Why not write to her, saying that some of her money is in danger of being lost, and that she must return at once in order to take the necessary steps to save it?"

"By Jove, but that's a good idea!" ejaculated Frederic Vernon. "Remington, you have a long head on you. I'll write the letter at once."

"You must be very careful how you word it, otherwise she may smell a mouse, as the saying is."

"Yes, I'll look her interests up first and find out how they stand. I had a list which I kept after giving up being her secretary."

"Then you ought to be able to compose a first-rate letter."

"But how will I send it? I am not supposed to know where she is."

"Tell her you saw the notice in the newspaper."

"To be sure--I didn't think of that."

On returning to his bachelor apartments Frederic Vernon looked over the papers he had kept, which should have been turned over to Robert, and found that his aunt owned thirty thousand dollars' worth of stock of the Great Lakes Lumber Company, whose principal place of business was in Chicago. This stock had once dropped, but was now worth a little above par value.

"This will do," he murmured to himself, and sitting down to his desk, penned the following letter:

"My Dearest Aunt:

"I was very much surprised to learn about a week ago that you had left Chicago for parts unknown. I suppose you are off on a little trip, and do not want to be worried about business or anything else. I thought you were in California, and was much surprised to see, by the New York Herald, that you are in London.

"I called at your home to tell you about the Great Lakes Lumber Company. Quite by accident I overheard a talk between the president of the concern and some stockholders, and learned that they intend to freeze out some of the other stockholders, including yourself. I heard the president say, 'We'll get that woman out, even if we don't get anybody else out.'

"Under such conditions, I would advise you to return to Chicago at once, and then I will tell you all of the details, so that you can proceed against the company without delay and save yourself.

"I am in the best of health, and about to accept a fine business opening with one of the leading railroads. I trust you are also well, and that your ocean trip does you a world of good.

"Devotedly your nephew,
"Frederic Vernon."

"There, what do you think of that?" asked Vernon of Remington, when the two met on the following morning.

"It's pretty strong," was the physician's answer. "If the president of that company got hold of the letter he could make you sweat for it."

"But he shan't get hold of it. As soon as my aunt comes back, I'll confiscate the letter,--and I'll look to you to do the rest."

"I am ready to do all I can. If we work the deal properly, we'll have her in a private asylum inside of forty-eight hours after she returns."

The letter was duly addressed to Mrs. Vernon, in care of the Charing Cross Hotel, London, and Frederic carried it down to the post-office so that it might start on its long journey without delay.

"I suppose I'll have to wait at least two weeks now," said Vernon dolefully. "It's a long time, but it cannot be helped."

He was waiting patiently for the time to come when he might draw his allowance from Mr. Farley.

Promptly on the day it was due he called at the lawyer's office.

He expected seven hundred and fifty dollars--a quarter of his yearly allowance of three thousand dollars, but instead, Mr. Farley offered him a hundred and fifty dollars.

"Why, what does this mean?" demanded the young man, who could scarcely believe the evidence of his eyesight.

"You ought to know better than I, Mr. Vernon," replied the lawyer quietly.

"Don't I get my usual allowance?"

"No; Mrs. Vernon has instructed me to give you a hundred and fifty dollars monthly after this."

"Why, that is only eighteen hundred a year!"

"You are right, sir."

"But I was getting three thousand."

For answer to this Mr. Farley merely shrugged his shoulders.

"It is an outrage!" went on the young man.

"If you don't want to take the money you don't have to," said the lawyer coldly. He was utterly disgusted with Frederic Vernon's manner.

"I'll have to take it," groaned Vernon. "But how I am to live on a hundred and fifty a month I don't know."

"At your age I would have been glad to have had half that amount per month, Mr. Vernon."

"You were not in society as I am, Mr. Farley."

"You are right there--and I am glad of it."

"I don't think my aunt has any right to cut me down in this fashion."

"Is she called upon to allow you anything?"

The shot told, and Frederic Vernon's face grew red.

"I am her nearest relative."

"I know that."

"Blood ought to count for something."

"I agree with you."

"I have always done my best to further my aunt's interests."

"You were her secretary for awhile, I believe."

"I was, until she took in an upstart of a boy in my place."

"Young Frost seems to be a nice young man."

"He is a snake in the grass. He has prejudiced my aunt against me."

"I know nothing about that."

"Then you cannot possibly let me have more money?" asked Vernon, as he arose to go.

"No; I cannot. Will you sign for the check or not?"

"I will sign," was the desperate answer, and, having done so, the young man took the check and hurried off with it.

"Matters have come to a pretty pass," he hissed between his set teeth when on the street once more. "Who knows but what she'll soon cut me off altogether. I hope she comes home as soon as she gets my letter, and that we get her into a private asylum without any trouble."

CHAPTER XII.
AN UNEXPECTED RESULT.

"Two letters for you, Mrs. Vernon," said Robert, as he came to the lady one fine day after a drive in the park.

"Thank you, Robert," she replied, and gazed at the writing on the envelopes. "I declare one is from my nephew Frederic!"

"Why, I thought he didn't know where you were," replied the youth.

"I wasn't aware that he did know. I told nobody but Mr. Farley."

"Then perhaps the lawyer told him," suggested our hero.

"No, Mr. Farley is too discreet for that. The second letter is from him."

Without delay Mrs. Vernon opened Frederic's communication and read it. Robert saw by her face that she was greatly perplexed.

"This is too bad!" she murmured.

"No bad news, I hope, madam?" said Robert.

"It is bad news. Read the letter for yourself," and Mrs. Vernon passed it over.

While Robert read Vernon's letter, the lady perused the communication from her lawyer. It was on several matters of business, but one passage will certainly interest the reader.

> "I have followed your directions and had your nephew watched," wrote Mr. Farley. "He is very thick with Dr. Remington, and the pair seem to have some plot between them. Will write again in a few days."

"Well, Robert, what do you think of Frederic's letter?" asked Mrs. Vernon, as she put her lawyer's epistle away.

"Do you want me to speak frankly?" replied our hero.

"Certainly."

"Then let me say that I think it is merely a ruse to get you to come home."

"Do you really think so?"

"I do. Your nephew knows he can do nothing while you are out of his reach."

"I have thought of that--in fact, that is why I came to England. If I go back, what do you suppose he will do?"

"Hire that Dr. Remington to put you into an asylum, and then try to get control of your money."

"Then you do not advise me to go back?"

"No, indeed; at least, not until you have proved to your own satisfaction that what he writes is true."

"I might get Mr. Farley to investigate."

"Then that is just what I was going to suggest. As he is authorized to transact all business for you, he can probably do as much as if you yourself were on the ground."

"Yes, I know, but----" Mrs. Vernon paused and flushed up.

"You hate to expose your family affairs, even to Mr. Farley," interposed Robert. "That is too bad, certainly, but I don't see how it can be helped. Sooner or later the truth must come out."

"I am willing to let Mr. Farley know all--in fact, he knows a good deal already. But the world at large----"

"Then tell Mr. Farley to investigate in private. One thing is sure, I wouldn't go back if I were you."

"I don't know but what you are right, Robert. But, oh, it is terrible to think one's relative is so treacherous," concluded Mrs. Vernon, and she could scarcely keep from weeping.

Robert did his best to cheer her up, and then she sat down and dictated a long letter to Mr. Farley, asking him to investigate the charge against the Great Lakes Lumber Company without delay. This letter Robert posted before going to bed.

Although rather strong appearing, Mrs. Vernon was in reality quite a delicate woman, and worrying over her nephew's doings soon told on her. She grew pale, and hardly ate at all when she came to the table. Robert was quick to notice the change.

"London air doesn't seem to agree with you," he remarked one morning. "Don't you think a change might be of benefit?"

"I was considering the question of leaving the city," replied the lady. "Perhaps it would be as well for us to take quarters in some pretty town up the Thames. I would like to find some place where the driving and boating are both good."

"I am sure it will be an easy matter to obtain what we want if we hunt around a little," said Robert.

A few days later they left London and removed to Windsor, where the royal palaces are located. Here they remained two days, and then settled down at a pretty town which I shall call Chishing, located on a small bluff overlooking the Thames at a point where the river was both wide and beautiful.

Their new boarding place was a pretty two-and-a-half story affair, with a long, low parlor, and an equally long and low dining hall. It was kept by Mrs. Barlow, a stout, good-natured English woman, who did all in her power to make her visitors comfortable. They had two rooms, which, while they did not connect, were still side by side, and both overlooked the river, and a pretty rose garden besides.

"I know I shall like it here," said Mrs. Vernon, as she sat by the window of her apartment, drinking in the scene one day at sunset. "Robert, what do you think?"

"I will like it, too, for awhile."

"I suppose you are thinking of home."

"I must admit I am. To tell the truth, I am afraid my mother is not very happy."

"I fear you are right." Mrs. Vernon sighed. "With your mother, it is her husband, while with me, it is my nephew. Ah, if only everything in this world would go right for once!"

"Well, we have to take things as they come, and make the best of them," replied our hero.

The next day there was a letter for him from his mother. In this Mrs. Talbot mentioned his communications, and told how she had come to let her husband have the thirteen thousand dollars. She concluded by stating that she was afraid she had made a big mistake.

"I am certain she has made a big mistake," said Robert to himself. "Mr. Talbot will never give the money back, and I know it. I think she is doing enough by supporting him. I don't believe he has done a stroke of work since he was sick."

Robert soon felt at home, and on the third day went down to the river to take a row, a pastime of which he had been fond while at home.

As he passed to the dock where boats could be hired, he ran plump into a red-headed boy named Sammy Gump. Sammy was strong and heavy set, and had been the bully of Chishing for several years.

"Hullo, Yankee, where are you going?" he demanded, as he pushed Robert roughly.

"I am going to attend to my own business," replied our hero quietly. "Have you any objection?"

"Dreadful fine clothes you have got; oh, dear!" smirked Sammy. "We are dressed for the ball, we are!"

"Let me pass," demanded Robert, and tried to go around the bully, who suddenly pushed him, and tried to trip him in the dust of the road.

But for once Sammy Gump had reckoned without his host, for although he sent Robert staggering several yards, our hero did not fall.

Gump expected Robert to beat a retreat, and was taken aback when the boy came forward with clenched fists.

"What do you mean by treating me like that?" demanded Robert.

"Oh, go along with you!" howled the bully. "If you don't like it, do the other thing."

"You are mighty impudent about it."

"Am I?" sneered Sammy. "Say, Yankee, how do you like that?"

And he slapped Robert on the cheek.

If our hero was surprised that instant, the bully was more surprised the instant after, for hauling back, Robert let fly with his fist, and took Sammy Gump fairly and squarely in the mouth, a direct blow that landed the bully flat on his back and loosened two of his teeth.

"Wh--what did yo--you do that for?" he spluttered, as after an effort he arose and glared at Robert.

"To teach you a lesson, you overgrown bully," replied Robert. "The next time, I imagine, you will know enough to leave me alone." And then he passed along to the dock to hire the rowboat.

Sammy Gump glared after him in baffled rage. "All right; you just wait," he muttered. "Nobody ever struck me yet but what he didn't rue it afterward!"

CHAPTER XIII.
VERNON'S HIGH-HANDED PROCEEDINGS.

Frederic Vernon found it very hard to cut down his expenses. He had so accustomed himself to luxurious living that to give up any of the good things of life was to him worse than having a tooth pulled.

Yet it was absolutely necessary that he do something, for his rent was due, and his tailor had threatened to sue him unless at least a part of the bill for clothing was paid.

Returning from Mr. Farley's office he found his landlord waiting for him.

"Good-morning, Mr. Vernon," said the landlord stiffly. "I called for the quarter's rent for your apartments."

"I am very sorry, Mr. Brown," replied Vernon smoothly. "But I will have to ask you to wait until next week. My banker----"

"I can't wait any longer, Mr. Vernon," was the quick rejoinder. "You promised to settle to-day."

"Yes, but my banker disappointed me, and----"

"Then you cannot pay?"

"No."

"Then I am ordered by the owner of the building to serve you with a notice to quit," said Mr. Brown quietly.

At this Frederic Vernon was thunderstruck. He, one of the leading society lights of the city, served with a notice to quit his bachelor apartments! It was preposterous, scandalous!

"Mr. Brown, do you know who I am?" he demanded, drawing himself up to his full height.

"Certainly. Mr. Frederic Vernon."

"Exactly, sir, and a member of one of our first families, sir."

"I can't help that, sir. The owner of this building expects his money from the first family tenants as well as from the others."

"You are--er--a--a----"

"No use to quarrel about it, Mr. Vernon. You must pay, or I will serve the notice."

A wordy war followed, but Mr. Brown was obdurate, and to avoid being set out on the street Frederic Vernon paid him fifty dollars on account, and promised to settle the balance inside of ten days. Then the young man walked into his parlor, threw himself into an easy chair, lit a Havana cigar, and gave himself up to his reflections.

But not for long, for five minutes later there was a knock on the door and opening it, he found himself confronted by Mr. Simon Moses, his tailor.

"Ver sorry, inteet, to disturb you, Mr. Vernon," said the tailor, who was a Hebrew, "but I come to see if you vould pe so kind as to bay up dot pill you vos owin' me for der last seex months."

"No; I haven't got any money now," growled Vernon. "Come next week."

"Dot is oxactly vot you say las' veek, und de veek pefore, Mr. Vernon. Dot pill is long oferdue, and I vos need mine monish."

"So do I need my money, but I can't get it, Mr. Moses. I've got six thousand dollars owing me for a month, and can't get a cent of it."

For the moment the Hebrew was astonished, then a crafty look came into his eyes.

"Maype you vill sign ofer von of dem claims to me, hey?" he suggested. "Chust enough to cofer mine pill, see?"

"No, I can't do that. Call in ten days and I will pay up in full."

"Dot is positive?"

"Do you doubt the word of a gentleman?"

"Very vell, I vill call chust ten days from to-day. And if you no bay up den, I will go and see your rich aunt about dot pill." And with this parting shot Simon Moses left the apartments, banging the door after him. Going to the door, Vernon locked it.

"Nobody else shall disturb me," he thought, and sat down to finish his smoke. "So he will go to my aunt, eh? Ha! ha! I guess he'll have something of a job to locate her, especially if Martha tells him she is in California."

The days passed, and Vernon waited impatiently for a letter from his aunt. He felt almost certain that she would write, stating she would be back by the first available steamer. When the time was past and no letter came, he began to grow suspicious.

"Perhaps she didn't get the letter," suggested Dr. Remington. "She may have left Charing Cross Hotel, you know."

"More than likely young Frost got the letter and destroyed it," answered Vernon. "I should have sent it in care of Mr. Farley. He may have some secret way of communicating with her."

"Well, don't worry too much. You may get a letter before the week is out," concluded Remington, and there the matter dropped and the two sallied off to waste several hours in drinking and in playing billiards. Remington had no visible means of support, but managed to squeeze out a living by sponging from those who were richer than himself. It was true he now got very little out of Vernon, but he was living in the hope that the plan against the rich aunt would be carried through, and he would become ten thousand dollars richer by the operation.

The mail steamer had brought no letter for Vernon, but it had brought a very important communication for Mr. Farley, and after reading it carefully the lawyer decided to act without delay. He was acquainted with Richard Anderson, the president of the Great Lakes Lumber Company, fairly well, and knew him to be a pillar of the church and in sound financial standing.

With proper delicacy the lawyer approached the subject at hand, and Richard Anderson listened in amazement.

"It is absurd to think there is anything wrong with our company, Mr. Farley," said the gentleman, with spirit. "If Mrs. Vernon thinks so all she has to do is to put her stocks on the market, and I will buy them up at two per cent. above par value. How did such a silly rumor ever reach her ears?"

"I hardly feel justified in stating how the rumor started."

"But I must demand it of you, Mr. Farley. Why, such a report, if it spread, might do our company a tremendous harm."

"I agree with you on that point."

"Tell me the truth, and I will see that you do not suffer through it."

"I do not want Mrs. Vernon to suffer."

Richard Anderson thought for a moment, then leaped to his feet.

"Tell me, did that report come from that fool of a nephew of hers?" he demanded.

"What makes you think it might come from him?"

"Because I heard that he was angry at her for leaving Chicago and not letting him know where she had gone to. The young fool let it out at one of the clubs when he was half full of liquor."

"Well, if you must know, it did come from Vernon. But don't let on that I told you," said the lawyer.

"The scoundrel! Farley, do you know what I think of doing?"

"Don't have him arrested. It will break Mrs. Vernon's heart."

"I won't. But I'm going to thrash him within an inch of his life, the puppy!"

"You can do as you see fit on that score." And Mr. Farley could not help but smile.

"Where does he live, with his aunt?"

"No, he has bachelor quarters at the Longmore."

"Very well. He shall hear from me before to-morrow night. I'll take some of his baseness out of him."

"Don't get yourself into trouble," was Mr. Farley's warning as he arose to go.

"Oh, I won't murder him, rest easy about that," returned Richard Anderson grimly.

On his way home that night he stopped at a harness store and asked to see the whips.

"I want something short, and with a good, stinging lash," he said.

"Got a bad horse to deal with, eh?" said the salesman.

"Yes, the worst colt in the city."

"All right, sir, here you are. That will fetch him, I'll warrant you."

"How much?"

"One dollar."

"That will do." Richard Anderson paid the money and had the whip wrapped up.

"Now, Frederic Vernon, I'll wager I'll make you face the music to-morrow," he muttered, as he took a car for home. "If I don't lay this on well it will be because I've forgotten how, and I guess a man don't forget these things very easily."

CHAPTER XIV.
VERNON'S UNWELCOME VISITOR.

When another day had passed and no letter came to Frederic Vernon, the young man began to grow desperate.

"I've got to raise money somehow," he said to himself.

But the question was a difficult one to settle, since he had already used his friends as much as he dared.

He was a late riser, and it was after ten o'clock when he was preparing to go out to a nearby restaurant for breakfast, when there came a hasty knock on his door.

He was expecting Remington, and unlocked the door without a second thought--to find himself confronted by Richard Anderson. The face of the capitalist was stern, and in one hand he carried the horsewhip he had recently purchased.

"Well, Vernon, I reckon you did not expect to see me," said the president of the lumber company coldly.

"Why--er--no, I did not," stammered the young man.

"I want to have a little talk with you, young man."

"Yes, sir," answered Vernon, with a shiver. "What--er--what about?"

"I want to know why you have been circulating a report calculated to hurt our lumber company."

"Me?" cried Vernon, pretending to be astonished.

"Yes, you."

"I have circulated no report."

"It is useless for you to deny it, young man. I have it upon the best authority that the report came from you."

"What report?"

"That our company was in a bad way financially and liable to go to pieces at any time."

As Richard Anderson finished he closed and locked the door and placed the key in his pocket.

"Hi! what are you doing that for?" gasped Frederic Vernon in alarm.

"So that nobody can interrupt me while I am teaching you a lesson."

"I--I don't understand."

"You will understand when I begin to use this horsewhip."

Vernon grew white and trembled so that he could scarcely stand up.

"You won't dare to--to hit me," he faltered.

"Won't I? You just wait and see. Do you know that I could have you arrested for what you have done?"

"I deny doing anything."

"And I can prove what you have done. If it wasn't for that kind-hearted aunt of yours I would let you go to prison."

"Did Mrs. Vernon tell you what I--I mean did she accuse me?" ejaculated the young man, so astonished that he partly forgot himself.

"No, she hasn't told me anything that you may have written to her. My information came from an outside party who happened to be my friend. But your slip just now proves what my friend told me. You are a rascal, Vernon, but instead of having you locked up, I am, for your aunt's sake, going to take it out of your hide."

As Richard Anderson concluded he threw back his arm, and down came the lash of the horsewhip across Vernon's shoulder.

"Ouow!" yelled the young man. "Oh, murder! Stop! stop! I'll be cut to pieces!"

Swish! swish! swish! down came the horsewhip again and again, over Vernon's shoulders, his back, around his legs, and one cut took him around the neck and face. The lumber dealer was thoroughly in earnest, and though the young man tried to fight him off it was useless.

"I will have you arrested for this!" shrieked Vernon, as he danced around with pain. "Oh, my neck! Oh, my legs! Stop! stop!"

"I hope this proves a lesson you never forget," returned Richard Anderson, with a final cut over Vernon's quivering back. "And now take my advice, and don't go to law over it, for if you do I shall expose you and make you pay the full penalty of your evil doings."

"I'll--I'll kill you when I get the chance!" roared Vernon, in a wild rage.

"No, you won't touch me. You just behave yourself, and stop being a fool and a spendthrift, and perhaps you'll get along better."

With these final words Richard Anderson unlocked the door again and walked out, taking his whip with him. As soon as the lumber dealer had departed Vernon closed the door, and not only locked but bolted it, and then sank into an easy chair, the picture of misery and despair.

"Oh, the rascal," he groaned, as he nursed his cuts, which smarted like fire. "I won't get over this in a month!" He gazed into a handy looking-glass. "Everybody at the club will ask where I got that cut on the neck and cheek. I wish I could kill him, yes, I do!"

But his rage, although intense, was useless, and after a while he cooled down a little, and then set to work to bathe his cuts and put something soothing on them. During this time there was a knock on the door, at which Vernon instantly became quiet.

"Hullo, Frederic, are you asleep yet?" came in Dr. Remington's voice.

"He mustn't see me in this condition," thought the young man, and continued quiet.

There followed another knock and a pause. "Guess he's out for breakfast," muttered the doctor, and stalked away.

"Breakfast," murmured Vernon. "I don't feel as if I could eat a mouthful in a week."

For the thrashing had made him sick all over. It was nearly noon when he did venture out, and then he got his first meal of the day at a restaurant where he was unknown.

He wondered greatly who had informed Richard Anderson of what was going on. Strange to say, he never suspected Mr. Farley.

"It must have been that Robert Frost," he said, at last. "He has read my letter to aunt, and wants to get me into trouble. I wish he was at the bottom of the ocean!"

All day long Vernon brooded over the way he had been treated.

"If this whole affair comes out and aunt hears of it, she will treat me worse than ever," he reasoned. "I wish I could get to her and have a talk." He felt certain that he would be able to persuade Mrs. Vernon into treating him more liberally, not suspecting that she had discovered the plot to send her to an insane asylum.

At last a bold, bad plan entered his head, and he resolved to act upon it the very next morning. He would draw up a check for himself for six hundred dollars, and sign Mrs. Vernon's name to it. He was a clever penman, and felt he could imitate her signature closely. He had frequently received large checks from her, and the forgery would never be suspected at the bank.

His first move was to get the necessary blank check at the bank. This was easy, as such blanks are always to be found on the desks provided for the use of the public.

Having obtained several blanks he hurried home and brought out a number of letters Mrs. Vernon had written. With these as a guide to the style of writing, he filled in one of the blanks and signed her name. Then, from his knowledge of her private business, he filled in the number, making it high enough to clear all checks below it. His first effort was a complete success, and so he threw the other blanks away.

Noon found him again at the bank, and having endorsed the check with his own name he walked to the window and asked to have it cashed. The teller knew him, and passed out the six hundred dollars without comment.

When Vernon found himself on the sidewalk it must be confessed that the cold perspiration stood out on his forehead. He was a high-handed criminal, and he knew it. For what he had done the law could send him to state's prison for a long term of years.

"And now to get away from Chicago, and from the United States," he told himself, and took a hack for his bachelor apartment. Once in the rooms, he packed his trunk and valise and donned a traveling suit. Before night he was on his way to New York, and forty-eight hours later he had secured passage on an ocean liner for England.

CHAPTER XV.
A FIGHT AND A FIRE.

To go rowing on the River Thames became a favorite amusement with Robert, and many an hour was spent thus, when Mrs. Vernon did not need him.

Occasionally the lady would go with our hero, but she was now suffering from rheumatism, and the dampness affected her so that she soon preferred to remain in the cozy boarding house.

"But do not remain in on my account, Robert," she said one day, on declining his suggestion to go out. "A boy like you needs all the fresh air and exercise he can get."

"I hate to go and leave you alone," he replied.

"You are with me enough. While you are gone I shall do a little fancy work and read, and perhaps lie down for a nap."

Secretly Mrs. Vernon was much worried over the outcome of her letter to Mr. Farley concerning Frederic's communication, but she did not let on to her young secretary.

"It will do no good," she thought. "There is already enough trouble as it is."

There was a brisk wind blowing when Robert made his way to the dock where he usually hired his boat, but otherwise the day promised to be a perfect one.

Our hero generally obtained his craft from an old tar named Jack Salter, but on reaching the landing place he was disappointed to find Salter nowhere in sight.

"He must have gone out to fish," he said to himself. "I wonder if I dare take a boat without asking him? I suppose it will be all right."

He was looking the boats over when suddenly several big boys came rushing out of a building nearby and surrounded him. The leader of the crowd was Sammy Gump, the bully of the village.

"Hi, there!" bawled Sammy. "What are you doing among Jack Salter's boats?"

"I was going to hire one," answered Robert quietly, although he did not like the looks of the crowd that surrounded him.

"Hire one?" sneered Sammy. "It's more than likely you were going to take one without hiring it."

Robert's face flushed and his eyes blazed as he faced the bully.

"Do you mean to say that I was going to steal one?" he demanded.

"Never mind what I meant. You leave Jack Salter's boats alone."

"I believe I have as much right here as you."

"Hear him!" sneered several. "Don't the Yankee think he's big!"

"Jack Salter isn't going to let you have any more boats," put in Bob Snipper, who was Sammy Gump's particular toady.

"And why not?"

"Because we told Jack not to," answered Sammy Gump. "We haven't any boats for such fellows as you."

"I think Jack Salter will let me have all the boats I want if I pay for them," returned Robert sharply. "Anyway, this is a public dock and a public business, and you have no right to interfere with my affairs."

"Don't you talk like that, or you'll catch it," growled Sammy.

"From you?" answered Robert quickly. "Perhaps you have forgotten our encounter of the other day."

"You took an unfair advantage of me then," went on the bully. "I'm going to teach you a lesson for it."

He made a signal to his companions and of a sudden all of the English boys hurled themselves upon our hero.

Robert was not expecting such a combined attack, and before he could save himself he was down on his back, with three of his tormentors on top of him.

"Now give it to him, fellows!" cried Sammy. "Pound him as hard as you can!"

"Not much!" answered Robert, as he let out with his foot. The blow landed on the bully's knee and made him howl with pain.

But Robert could not throw the others off at once, and they hit him half a dozen times. At last he got up with a quick side movement, and hauling off he hit Bob Snipper such a blow that the toady lost his balance and went backward with a loud splash into the river.

"Bob's overboard!" was the cry. "He'll be drowned!"

"Save me! save me!" yelled Snipper. "I--I can't swim!" And then throwing up both arms he disappeared from view.

"You've killed him!" cried Sammy hoarsely.

"He had no right to attack me," answered Robert. "But he is not dead yet, and I think we can get him ashore if we hurry."

He leaped from the dock into the nearest boat. As he cast off he looked at the others, expecting one or more to follow him to the rescue, but nobody volunteered. Nearly all were too dazed to act.

Snipper had gone down, and when he came up it was fully twenty feet from where the boat rode. Seizing an oar, Robert paddled toward the unfortunate youth.

"Keep up!" he cried encouragingly. "I will help you in half a minute!"

Bob Snipper saw Robert approaching and it gave him a little hope. He had forgotten all about how badly he had treated our hero. He made a clutch at the oar Robert extended toward him, and having secured a firm hold was quickly drawn aboard of the rowboat.

"Now, I guess you are all right," said Robert, who was hardly excited at all.

"I--I--suppose I am," gasped the bully's toady. "I--I--am much obliged to you for hauling me out of the water."

"So you got him out, eh?" remarked Sammy, as Robert paddled back to the dock.

"Yes."

"It wasn't much to do. I would have gone for him myself if you had given me the chance."

"There was no time to waste," was Robert's brief reply. "Come, you can jump ashore now," he added, to his dripping passenger.

"Aren't you coming ashore?" said Snipper slowly.

"No, I am going out on the river. I don't think any of you will stop me from using this boat now."

"You can take it so far as I am concerned," answered the bully's toady, with a face full of shame. "I shan't set myself up against you again, I can tell you that!"

"Yes, go on and take the boat, Frost," put in one of the other boys. "You're the right sort, and I'm sorry we attacked you."

One of the other boys also spoke up, expressing his regrets at the encounter. But Sammy Gump remained silent, his face just as sour as before.

"I'm awfully thankful he pulled me out," said Bob Snipper, after Robert had left the vicinity of the dock. "If he hadn't I would have been drowned."

"That's right, Bob," said one of the others.

"Humph!" muttered Sammy. "You are trying to make a regular hero out of him, when he is nothing of the sort."

"Well, why didn't you come and pull me out?" asked Bob.

"I was going to--but he got ahead of me."

"I can't swim, and it wouldn't have taken me long to drown, I can tell you that."

"He did very well," said another lad of the crowd. "After this I am going to be friendly with him."

"All right, Dick Martin, do as you please. I'll never be friendly with him," answered Sammy Gump, and strode away in as bad a humor as ever.

As Bob Snipper was soaked to the skin, there was nothing for him to do but to either go home and change his clothes, or else go bathing and let his suit dry in the meantime.

Afraid of a scolding if he went home, the boy concluded to go bathing, and Dick Martin and one other lad accompanied him, while the others hurried away after Sammy Gump.

"I don't believe the American boy is half a bad sort," said Dick Martin, as the three moved up the Thames to where there was a tiny inlet well screened with trees and bushes. "He had a perfect right to hire a boat if he wanted it and could pay for it."

"We made a big mistake to follow Sammy into the game," said Harry Larkly, the third boy. "Sammy was mad at him because of a row the two had on the road some time ago."

"After this I am going to treat him as a friend," said Dick Martin. "It's all tom-foolery to give him the cold shoulder just because he's an American. Why, I've got half a dozen cousins in America."

"So have I," put in Bob Snipper. "And when my father went to Boston last year the folks over there treated him first-rate. We were fools to let Sammy lead us around by the nose."

"Well, we'll know better next time," said Harry Larkly. "If Sammy won't do the right thing by him, why, I'm going to cut Sammy, that's all."

The swimming place was soon gained, and having placed his garments in the sun to dry, Bob Snipper went in for a second bath, but this time taking very good care not to go out over his depth.

The others soon followed, and went out a considerable distance, for both were good swimmers.

"Why can't you swim, Bob?" asked Dick.

"I don't know, I'm sure. Every time I try my head goes down like a lump of lead."

"That's queer."

"My brother is the same way--and my father says he could never learn either."

"It must run in the family," said Harry, with a grin. "Like wooden legs among soldiers. I think you can learn if you'll only try and keep cool. You get too excited."

The boys remained in the water for nearly an hour. By this time the wind and the sun had about dried Bob's garments, and then all began to dress.

"Hullo, what's that?" cried Dick suddenly, as he pointed toward the village. "See the heavy smoke."

"It's some place on fire!" burst out Bob. "I wonder what place it can be?"

All three boys ran toward the river road, putting on the last of their garments on the way.

"It's Mrs. Barlow's boarding house!" ejaculated Dick Martin. "Say, fellows, this wind is going to sweep the house to the ground!"

"Mrs. Barlow's?" repeated Harry Larkly. "Why, that is where that American boy and his lady companion board."

"That's so, Harry," said Bob. "And that is where Norah Gump, Sammy's sister, works, too," he added. "I hope none of those people are in danger of being burnt up."

CHAPTER XVI.
ROBERT SHOWS HIS BRAVERY.

Robert was hardly in a fit mental condition to enjoy his row, and his face was very serious as he drew away from the crowd that had molested him.

"I don't see what they want to act so for?" he mused, as he pulled up the broad stream. "I never tried to harm any of them, or interfered with their amusements."

Crossing to the other side of the Thames he started to fish for a while.

But the fish were not biting well just then, and after bringing up one small stickleback, a fish very common to England's streams, he drew in his lines and gave it up.

Close to where the rowboat rode was a grassy bank, filled with moss and several species of ferns, and presently Robert jumped ashore to investigate.

"Those ferns are very pretty," he thought. "I guess I'll dig some up, put them in a flowerpot and place them in one of our windows. I am certain Mrs. Vernon will be pleased to watch them grow."

He was prowling around, and had already dug up half a dozen ferns and some moss to wrap them in, when he discovered the smoke drifting over the village.

"That looks pretty close to our boarding house," he said to himself. "Can it be possible that it is Mrs. Barlow's place?"

Much alarmed, he leaped into his boat and seized the oars. A few strokes took him well out into the stream, and then he made out that it was the boarding house beyond the possibility of a doubt.

With desperate energy he began to row for the nearest landing to the house.

"If only Mrs. Vernon is safe," he said to himself, over and over again.

He knew only too well how badly she was suffering from rheumatism, and also knew that at this time of day she was probably lying down trying to catch a nap.

At last the landing was gained, and our hero leaped from the boat and ran at top speed for the boarding house.

By this time the alarm had been given through the village, and the inhabitants were hurrying to the scene of the conflagration from all directions.

There was but one fire engine in the place, and this was a very primitive affair, so, with such a strong wind blowing, it was speedily seen that Mrs. Barlow's resort was doomed.

When Robert came up he ran plump into the landlady, who was rushing out of the house with a lamp in one hand and a canary bird cage in the other.

"Mrs. Barlow, is Mrs. Vernon safe?" he asked breathlessly.

"Mrs. Vernon?" repeated Mrs. Barlow, in a semi-dazed fashion. "Sure, Mr. Frost, I don't know where she is."

Robert waited to hear no more, but ran into the boarding house and began to mount the stairs, three steps at a time.

"Mrs. Vernon!" he called out. "Mrs. Vernon, where are you?"

Getting no reply, he made his way through the upper hallway, which was rapidly filling with smoke. The fire was in the rear of the dwelling and so far the wind had blown it away, but now the wind was shifting and the fire was leaping from cellar to garret.

Robert, as we know, was naturally brave, and now the thought that the lady who had been so kind to him might be in peril of her life, lent him additional courage.

He tried Mrs. Vernon's door, to find it locked.

"Mrs. Vernon!" he repeated. "Mrs. Vernon!"

"What is it, Robert?" came sleepily from inside.

"Get up, quickly! The house is on fire!"

"On fire!" came with a gasp. "Oh, Robert!"

"Open the door and I will help you to get downstairs," went on the youth.

There was a hasty movement within the apartment and then the key turned in the lock. Robert threw the door open, to behold Mrs. Vernon standing before him, clad in a morning wrapper and her slippers.

Having just roused up from a sound sleep, she was bewildered and gazed at him questioningly.

"Come, there is no time to lose," he said, and took hold of her arm.

"My jewels and money----" she began, and pointed to the dresser. With one clutch he caught up the jewel case and her money box and placed them under his arm.

They hurried into the hallway. The smoke was now so thick that Robert could scarcely see the stairs. In her excitement Mrs. Vernon forgot all about her rheumatism. She clutched the young secretary tightly by the arm.

"Bend down and the smoke won't blind you so much," said Robert. "Lean on me if you are afraid of falling."

They passed downstairs as rapidly as the lady's condition permitted. In the lower hallway they again met Mrs. Barlow, along with several others, all carrying out furniture and other household effects.

Once outside, Robert conducted Mrs. Vernon to a place of safety, and set her down on a garden bench. She was still bewildered, but gradually her excitement left her.

The pair had hardly reached the bench when a piercing scream rang out, coming from the garret of the boarding house. At the small dormer window stood a young girl, waving her hands piteously for help.

"It is Norah Gump!" shouted somebody in the crowd. "What is she doing up there?"

"She went up for her bag of clothing," answered Mrs. Barlow. "She used to sleep in the garret."

Robert recognized the girl as one who had assisted the cook of the boarding house. He had heard her called Norah, but had never supposed that she was a sister to the bully of the village.

"She will be burnt up!" he cried, in horror.

"Oh, I trust not!" cried Mrs. Vernon. "See if you cannot aid her, Robert."

"I will," he returned, and dropping her jewel casket and her money box in her lap, he made again for the burning building.

"No use of trying to go up there," cried one of the firemen. "The stairs is burning already."

"Then why not get a ladder and put it up to the window?" asked Robert.

"Aint got no ladder," came from another man. "Maybe she had better jump."

"She'll break her neck if she jumps," said Robert. He looked up at the window and then at a tree which grew nearby. One of the branches of the tree was within four feet of the opening.

"Please save me!" shrieked the girl. "The room is full of smoke already!"

"Don't jump!" answered Robert. He turned to the firemen. "Give me a boost up into the tree."

"You can't reach the window from there," said one of the men.

"I think I can. But hurry, or it will be too late."

The firemen did as requested, and up the tree went Robert with the agility of a cat. He felt that it was a veritable climb for life.

The fire was now coming out of a parlor window, and this sent the smoke and sparks into the tree and up to the window at which the girl was standing.

"I can't stay here," moaned the girl, wringing her hands. "I must jump!" And she placed one foot on the window sill.

"Wait a few seconds longer," urged Robert, as he climbed nearer to her.

"The fire is coming up through the floor!"

With a jump, our hero gained the branch which grew out toward the window. Luckily it was a heavy limb, or it would not have sustained his weight. The end had originally pressed on the roof of the house, but this had been sawed off.

At last our hero was within four feet of the window sill, and somewhat below the opening. The girl watched him in a frenzy of terror. Buckling his feet under the tree limb Robert held out his arms.

"Now, jump and I will catch you," he said.

The girl needed no second bidding, for the flames were already licking the floor under her. Standing on the window sill she cast herself forth, and our hero caught and steadied her. It was no easy thing to do, and for one brief instant it looked as if both would fall to the ground. But Robert kept his hold, and soon they were safe and descending to the ground.

A cheer went up.

"He's a brave lad!" was the cry. "He deserves a medal!"

The women folks standing around said but little, yet all were deeply affected.

When Norah Gump reached the ground her emotions were such that she fainted dead away.

Restoratives were speedily applied, and while they were being administered Sammy Gump appeared on the scene, followed by the boys who had helped him in his attack on Robert.

"Is Norah dead?" he asked, in a quivering voice. He thought a good deal of his sister.

"No, she has only fainted from excitement," answered one of the women standing by. "She'll be all right in a little while. But she would have been burnt up if it hadn't been for that young gent yonder."

Sammy looked in the direction pointed out, and beheld Robert, who had rejoined Mrs. Vernon.

"Do you mean to tell me he saved her?" he demanded, in amazement.

"Yes, he did," put in one of the men, and gave the bully the particulars. These particulars were also corroborated by Bob Snipper and his chums.

"I can't understand it at all," said Sammy, a little while later, when he was taking his sister to his mother's house. "He's a good bit better chap than I dreamed he was."

CHAPTER XVII.
A DIAMOND SCARFPIN.

Robert found Mrs. Vernon resting comfortably on the garden bench. She smiled broadly when he came up.

"Robert, you are a regular hero," she observed. "Nobody could have done a braver deed."

"It was not so very much to do," he answered, with a blush. "I simply saw how the girl might be saved, and I set to work to do it."

"But it was no easy matter to catch the girl," went on the lady warmly. "You ran a big risk."

The firemen were now hard at work, and a steady stream of water was being poured on the conflagration. But the wind had caught the house fairly, and but little could be saved. Soon the men directed their efforts toward saving the adjoining property, and fortunately nothing but the boarding house was consumed.

As soon as the fire was over Mrs. Vernon and our hero set about finding another boarding place. This was an easy matter, for Mrs. Barlow's sister also took boarders. To Mrs. Cabe, therefore, they went, and procured rooms which were just as desirable as those which they had formerly occupied.

"It's too bad we couldn't save your trunks, Mrs. Vernon," observed Robert, after the boarding place question had been settled. "You've got only what you have on."

"Well, I am no worse off than you, Robert," she answered, with a peculiar smile.

"Oh, it doesn't matter so much for a boy."

"I suppose not. Still we both need outfits, and I shall see to it that we get them as soon as possible."

"There are not many stores in this town--I mean stores of any importance."

"We will take a journey to Oxford. We can get about all we want there, and it will give you a chance to look at the most celebrated English institutions of learning."

"I shall like that."

"You ought to have a college education, Robert. It would prove very useful to you. Not but what I am satisfied with you, however," added the lady hastily.

"I would like to go to Yale or Harvard first-rate."

"Perhaps we will be able to arrange that later." Mrs. Vernon paused for a moment. "Robert, I feel that I owe you a good deal for saving my life."

"You don't owe me anything, Mrs. Vernon. I did no more than my duty."

"I think otherwise. To free myself from pain I took a double dose of my medicine, and I was in an extra heavy sleep when you aroused me. If you had not come I would have slept on until it was too late."

And the lady closed her eyes for a moment and shuddered.

Taking her jewel case from her bureau drawer, Mrs. Vernon opened it and brought forth a neat but costly diamond scarf-pin.

"I am going to make you a present of this, Robert," she went on. "It will look very well on the new scarf I am going to purchase you."

"Oh, Mrs. Vernon, it is a diamond pin!"

"So it is, Robert."

"It must be worth a good deal of money."

"It cost me two hundred dollars at one of the leading Chicago jewelers. I don't mind telling you that I got the pin to give to Frederic on his birthday. But I have changed my mind about giving him a present."

"It's too valuable a gift for me to wear, Mrs. Vernon."

"Let me be the judge of that, Robert. Of course, you will be careful and not lose it."

"I'll take the best possible care of it," he answered, and then she gave it to him, and he thanked her heartily.

That evening after supper Mrs. Cabe came to Robert and told him that a boy was downstairs and wanted to see him very much. Robert went down and found Sammy Gump, who stood there hat in hand, and with a face full of shame.

"Excuse me for troubling you, Robert Frost," said the bully humbly. "But--but I wanted to thank you for saving Norah's life, and mother and father want me to thank you, too. They can't come themselves, because father's a stoker on the railway, and mother has got to stay home and take care of Norah."

"You are welcome to whatever I did, Gump," answered Robert. "I am glad I was of service."

"Did you know she was my sister?" asked Sammy curiously.

"No, I confess I did not."

"Oh!"

"But I would have saved her anyhow," added Robert hastily.

"Honest?"

"Yes, Gump, honest."

The bully of the town looked sharply into our hero's honest eyes, and his face grew redder than ever.

"I believe you; yes, I do," he observed, in a choking voice. "Say, do you know what? I'm awfully sorry I pitched into you. I was a big fool to do it. You're the right sort, and you'll never find me standing in your way again."

"I am glad to hear you talk so, Gump," answered Robert.

There was an awkward pause, and then our hero put out his hand. Sammy Gump clutched it eagerly and gave it a tight squeeze. From that instant the two boys were firm friends.

Nor was this all. Robert's generous action set Sammy Gump to thinking how mean and overbearing he had been, and the bully ended up by giving up all his overbearing manners, and treating everybody as he himself wished to be treated. He soon made a score of friends, and was as well liked as anybody in the town.

Two days later Robert and Mrs. Vernon set out for Oxford. The journey was a delightful one, and nightfall found them located at one of the principal hotels.

On the day following they went shopping, and Mrs. Vernon insisted upon having her young secretary measured for two business suits, a traveling suit, and also a dress suit, and likewise bought him a generous supply of other things to wear.

"As my private secretary, you must dress well," she said. "And I owe it to you to foot the bills myself."

"My old friends will hardly know me when they see me," said Robert, as he surveyed himself in one of his new suits. "I wonder what your nephew would say if he heard of this."

To this Mrs. Vernon did not reply, and quickly changed the subject. Little did they dream that Frederic Vernon was already on his way to see them.

Two more days were spent in Oxford, and Robert visited many places of interest, including several famous colleges, the cathedral, and the great library. Then Mrs. Vernon and our hero returned to Chishing.

"I am feeling ever so much better," she declared. "I believe the excitement of the fire and the traveling to Oxford helped me."

"I am glad of it," answered Robert. "But to have a fire to help a sick person is rather costly medicine."

At this Mrs. Vernon laughed outright. "Quite true, Robert, and I want no more fires. But we can travel. How would you like to go to Paris?"

"I will go anywhere you say, Mrs. Vernon."

"Paris is one of the most beautiful cities in the whole world. Perhaps we will go there before long."

"I am afraid my knowledge of French is rather limited," said our hero, with a faint smile.

"That will not matter much, since we can stop at an English hotel. I can speak French fluently."

"Have you any idea how long you will remain in Europe?"

"No, Robert. It will depend somewhat upon what Frederic does."

"It is queer that you do not get some word back from Mr. Farley."

"We may get a letter to-day."

Mrs. Vernon was right,--a letter came in the evening mail. In this the lawyer stated that he had investigated the charges brought against the Great Lakes Lumber Company, and found them to be utterly without foundation.

Mrs. Vernon grew very sober when she read the communication.

"What do you think of this?" she asked, after letting Robert read the letter.

"It is as I thought," answered the young secretary. "It was a ruse to get you back to the United States."

"Do you know what I feel like doing? I feel like writing to Mr. Farley to tell Frederic that he may expect no more remittances from me."

"If you cut him off entirely what will he do?"

"He will have to do as thousands of others do, go to work for a living."

"Does he know anything--I mean anything special?"

"He is an expert bookkeeper, and could get a position at that, if he would only apply himself."

On the day following Mrs. Vernon had some special business to be transacted in London, and sent Robert down to the metropolis to attend to it.

It was a fine day, and, left to herself, the lady prepared to go out for a short walk when a visitor was announced.

She went down to the parlor to see who it was, and was nearly struck dumb to behold Frederic Vernon.

CHAPTER XVIII.
VERNON PLAYS THE PENITENT.

"What, you!" cried Mrs. Vernon, when she could speak.

"Yes, aunt," replied Frederic Vernon awkwardly. "I suppose you didn't expect to see me."

"I certainly did not." And the lady sank in a chair.

"Aren't you going to shake hands with me?"

He came to her side and held out his hand, and she grasped it mechanically.

"When did you come over?" she asked.

"I arrived at Liverpool yesterday, and went directly to London. At the Charing Cross Hotel I found out that you had come here."

"I see."

She said no more, but stared hard at him.

"Dear aunt, cannot you forgive me," he said, trying to put on a sad face. "I have done wrong, I know, but I--I--couldn't help it."

"Sit down, Frederic, and tell me why you reported to me that the lumber company was in bad shape."

"Because I was told that it was a fact."

"Who told you that?"

"Some of the men at the Pioneer Club. They knew I, or rather you, were interested in the company."

"The report is absolutely false."

"So I have since heard, and I have come to you for the purpose of setting myself straight in your eyes."

Frederic Vernon had carefully rehearsed his part, and his manner was such that his aunt almost believed him.

"You wish to set yourself straight?" she asked slowly.

"Yes, dear aunt. I know I have done wrong, but I am not the rascal you may think I am."

"I have never said you were a rascal, Frederic."

"But you turned me away, and had that young Frost take my place."

"I did that because you neglected my business. Somebody had to attend to that business."

"And then you left Chicago without letting me know where you were going."

"I had my reasons for that."

"I trust you didn't do it on my account, aunt. I may have been neglectful, but I--well, I never tried to do you any harm, no matter what that young Frost or others may say against me." Frederic Vernon began to cough, and sank back on a sofa as if partly exhausted.

"You are not well?" she asked, in alarm.

"I am not very sick now. But I have been quite ill," he answered, telling the falsehood without a blush.

"And you have a scar on your neck and cheek."

"I was taken sick on the street, and fell down and cut myself on a stray barrel hoop," he answered. "But I guess I'll pull through."

Mrs. Vernon was alarmed, for he did look sick, and she at once began to question him about what he had done for himself.

"I haven't done much--I was too anxious to find you and set myself straight with you," he said. "Since you sent me off I have had no peace of mind at all."

"Perhaps I was a little hasty," said Mrs. Vernon, whose heart was a tender one. "You must consult a doctor at once, and settle down where you can have it comfortable."

The conversation between the pair lasted for fully an hour, and the upshot of the matter was that Mrs. Vernon engaged a room for Frederic at the boarding house opposite to that maintained by Mrs. Cabe, the latter resort being full.

"I will pay all of your expenses," she said. Then a doctor was ordered.

The physician was a man of small practice, and Frederic Vernon fooled him easily.

"He is, indeed, quite sick," said the doctor to Mrs. Vernon. "But rest and medicine will make him pull through, I feel certain of it." Then he wrote out a prescription, and a boy was sent to procure it at the apothecary shop. When the medicine came Frederic Vernon pretended to take it, but not a mouthful of it did he ever swallow.

"You'll not catch me swallowing any such dose," he said to himself, when he was alone, and poured the medicine out of the window.

He was highly elated over his success in fooling his aunt, and when left to himself felt like dancing a jig.

"I'll work my cards all right enough," he thought. "My next move must be to get rid of young Frost, and when my aunt takes me back I'll make sure that I am not thrown aside again."

Of course Robert was astonished to hear of Frederic Vernon's arrival. He listened gravely to what Mrs. Vernon had to tell him.

"It's too bad if he is sick, Mrs. Vernon," he said. "But take my advice and be careful how you trust him."

"I will be careful, Robert. But I am really afraid that I have been too hard on Frederic."

"Have you questioned him about that scheme he and Dr. Remington were hatching out?"

"No. I will bring that around when he is real well again."

"Of course he will deny it."

"It may be that you were mistaken, Robert."

"I don't think so."

It was not until two days later that Robert and Frederic Vernon met. In the meantime Mrs. Vernon had called upon her nephew a number of times.

"Glad to see you, Frost," said Frederic, extending his hand cordially. "I hear you are getting along first-rate as my aunt's private secretary."

"Thank you, I am doing very well," answered Robert stiffly. "How do you feel?"

"Oh, I am coming around slowly. But I've had a pretty bad spell of sickness."

"That isn't very nice."

"It's beastly. But sit down, I want to talk to you. How do you like things over here?"

"Oh, I am suited very well."

"Say, but that's a nice scarfpin you are sporting."

"It is a nice pin."

"Looks like a real diamond."

"It is."

"Where did you get it?"

"Mrs. Vernon gave it to me."

"You are in luck." Frederic Vernon laughed nervously. "By the way, I understand you have been playing the part of a hero."

"Who told you that?"

"The landlady here. She says you saved my aunt and a servant girl when that other boarding house burnt down."

"Well, I did what I could."

"You've lined your nest nicely," went on Frederic Vernon, eyeing Robert in a peculiar manner.

Robert's face flushed.

"What do you mean by that?"

"The first thing you know, Mrs. Vernon will be making you her heir."

"If she does it will be a complete surprise to me."

"Do you deny that you are working for that end?"

"I do deny it, most emphatically. I want no more than I am entitled to."

"Bah, you talk well, Frost, but don't think I can't see through your little plot. Has my aunt changed her will lately?"

"I don't know."

"You ought to know; you have charge of her private papers."

"I haven't seen anything of a will."

"Then she must have left it with Mr. Farley, in Chicago." And Frederic Vernon breathed a long sigh of relief.

He was very anxious to learn if his aunt had cut him off, but could get absolutely nothing out of Robert. If she had made no new will, however, the chances were that he was safe.

"How long is my aunt going to remain in England?" he went on.

"I cannot say. Why don't you ask her yourself?"

"I will. She left in a big hurry, didn't she?"

"I admit she did."

"What was the reason?"

"Perhaps you had better ask her that, too."

"Don't get saucy, Frost."

"I am not saucy. I wasn't hired to answer your questions."

"I want to be friends with you, not enemies. But you seem to wish otherwise."

"No, Mr. Vernon. But I am your aunt's private secretary, and it won't do for me to expose her business, or her motives for doing certain things."

Frederic Vernon looked daggers at Robert, but controlled himself.

"All right, as you please," he said carelessly. "But you may find it to pay to make a friend of me some day."

"I do not wish to be your enemy. But I must do my duty to your aunt," concluded Robert, and a minute later bowed himself away.

When our hero was gone Frederic Vernon grated his teeth.

"He's a clever one," he muttered. "But he shan't get the best of me. He knows all of her business, but he intends to keep it to himself. I must watch my chances and see if I cannot overhear what they talk about from time to time. Hang me, if I don't follow him now!"

And putting on his hat, Frederic Vernon did so. He saw Robert enter the garden attached to Mrs. Cabe's place and join Mrs. Vernon in the summerhouse overlooking the broad river. Taking care so that he would not be seen, he came up close to a tree near the summerhouse. From this point he could hear every word that passed between his aunt and our hero.

CHAPTER XIX.
MRS. VERNON'S BANK ACCOUNT.

"How did you find Frederic?" was Mrs. Vernon's first question when Robert joined her.

"He seems to be doing very well," answered the young secretary. "I don't think he was quite as sick as he made out to be."

"He was certainly sick when he came here. And he must have been very sick to fall and hurt himself on the neck and cheek."

"Perhaps you are right, Mrs. Vernon, I never had much to do with sick people."

"Did he ask you anything about yourself?"

"He asked me about the diamond scarfpin. I told him that you had given it to me."

"If Frederic really reforms I will get him one, too. What else did he ask about, Robert?"

"Well, he asked about you."

"And what did you say?"

"Maybe I had better not repeat our talk, Mrs. Vernon."

"Did you quarrel?"

"He was quite angry because I would not tell him about your will. He wanted to know if you had changed it lately."

"And what did you tell him?"

"That I knew nothing of a will."

Mrs. Vernon became thoughtful.

"I presume it would be a shame to cut him off," she said slowly.

"Have you done that?"

"Not yet. In my last will, which Mr. Farley holds, he is almost my sole heir. But I have been thinking of changing my will and leaving him only a quarter of my estate,--one-half of the whole estate to go to charitable institutions, and the remaining quarter to go to my friends, including yourself."

"I did not expect anything to be left to me, Mrs. Vernon. You have given me enough--in fact, more than enough--already."

"You have been like a son to me, Robert. But about Frederic--if he really and truly reforms, I think I will leave him the bulk of my fortune."

"I would not be too hasty. You see, I haven't forgotten the plot he and the doctor hatched against you."

"I will be very careful. I shall watch him for a year, and if during that time he does not reform thoroughly, I shall cut him off with a very small allowance, say a thousand dollars."

"A thousand dollars wouldn't be bad for most young fellows. But to him it will be nothing. By the way, he seems to have quite some money."

"I have noticed that, too, and it has puzzled me greatly, for, as you are aware, I have cut down his allowance."

"Perhaps somebody has loaned him some money."

"It is possible. But I know, through Mr. Farley, that he was in debt to many of his friends, and these folks will not go on loaning money forever."

"They may be banking on his prospects."

"Then they may get left, as the saying goes. I sincerely wish that Frederic would settle down to some business and make a man of himself."

Here the conversation changed, and soon after Mrs. Vernon went into the house, while Robert walked down to the river to take a row. Left to himself, Frederic Vernon stole back to his boarding quarters.

"So she will cut me off with a paltry thousand dollars unless I reform, eh, and she is going to watch me for a whole year," he muttered to himself. "I wonder when she will hear from that forged check? I hope it doesn't come in before I have time to arrange my future plans."

The more he thought of the matter, the more did the forged check worry him. He had hoped to get possession of his aunt's mail by applying at the local post-office, but this scheme had fallen through, as the mail was delivered only to Mrs. Vernon or to Robert, and orders were to deliver it to no one else.

Several days went by, and now Frederic came to see his aunt regularly morning, afternoon, and evening. From her he learned that she thought of going to Paris, and he eagerly favored the scheme, hoping that through the change he might be able to get the mail.

But he was doomed to bitter disappointment. Before any change could be made there came a long letter from Mr. Farley, showing how money matters stood. Among other things, this showed a deficiency in one bank account of six hundred dollars.

Robert looked over this communication with the lady, for this was a part of his work, Mrs. Vernon trusting him more and more every day with her private affairs.

"I cannot understand this," she said, after referring to her various bank accounts.

"Understand what, Mrs. Vernon?" he asked.

"The account at the American Exchange Bank is just six hundred dollars short."

"Are you certain the stubs have been footed up properly?" asked Robert, in much surprise.

"You footed them up yourself."

"So I did. But I will foot them up again."

The young secretary did so. "According to your check book, you have a balance there of two thousand and three hundred dollars," he said, when he had concluded his calculations.

"Exactly, and according to the bank rendering, made through Mr. Farley, the sum is seventeen hundred dollars--just six hundred dollars less. I cannot understand it."

Robert shook his head slowly, for he was as much puzzled as the lady.

"Let us look over the other accounts," he ventured. "Perhaps the money was transferred without a showing being made,--although I don't see how that could be."

There were six other bank accounts, running up to many thousands of dollars, but each was correct to the cent.

"You never drew a check and forgot to charge it up against the account, did you?" asked Robert.

"There is the book. Aren't all the stubs filled--I mean those from which the checks have been detached?"

Robert looked through the book with care.

"Yes, every one is filled out," he said.

"Then I don't understand it." Mrs. Vernon leaped to her feet suddenly. "Unless----" She stopped short.

"Unless----" repeated Robert, and then he, too, became silent. Both had thought of Frederic Vernon at the same time.

"I do not think he would do it," went on the lady, almost pitifully. "He has our family blood running in his veins. He would not be guilty of such a terrible crime."

Robert said nothing, but he had his own opinion of the nephew who would plot to put his aunt in the insane asylum just to get hold of her money.

"What do you advise, Robert?" she asked, as she began to pace the floor nervously.

"I would advise you to send to Chicago at once for an accounting from the bank, giving the numbers of the checks you have really issued. If you don't want the bank to know that something is wrong, transact the business through Mr. Farley."

"I will do so. I will send a cablegram to America this very day."

Mrs. Vernon set to work to prepare her cablegram with great care. Of course, the sending of such a message way off to Chicago would be expensive, but just now she did not think of the money, she wanted to know the truth concerning the shortage.

"If Frederic is guilty I will cut him off without a dollar," she said quietly, but so firmly that Robert felt she meant what she said.

Robert was commissioned to take the cablegram to the nearest telegraph office which could forward it, and on the way he met Frederic Vernon, who was out walking.

"Hullo, Frost, come and take a walk with me," said the young man patronizingly, as our hero approached.

"Thank you, but I just as lief walk alone," answered Robert shortly.

"Don't want to be sociable, eh? All right. Where are you bound?"

"That is my business."

"Humph!" Frederic Vernon stared at him for a moment. Then he walked on without further words. But at the corner he looked back and saw Robert enter the telegraph office.

"Something is in the wind," he muttered to himself, and retraced his steps. Getting behind several other people, he drew close to the youth and saw him send the message and pay a good round price for it.

"That message is going to Chicago, and I know it," he told himself, after following Robert to the road once more. "Now what did it contain? Has my aunt got wind of that forged check already? If so, I must act quickly, or my cake will be dough. Whatever comes, she must never live to alter her will."

All that night he brooded over the way matters had turned. He felt that he would be made a beggar did his aunt discover the forgery. But so far the only will she had made was in his favor. She must not be allowed to make another.

"I must watch her closely," he told himself. "She frequently goes out driving, and along the cliff back of the town, too. What if some day her team took fright and went over the cliff? I don't believe she would ever live to tell the tale, and the fortune would be mine!"

If Frederic Vernon was bitter against his aunt, he was also bitter against Robert, for he now knew that our hero had exposed the plot to get Mrs. Vernon into an insane asylum.

"He goes driving with her," thought the desperate man. "They can both go over the cliff together!"

CHAPTER XX.
THE RUNAWAY ALONG THE CLIFF.

The discovery of the shortage in her bank account made Mrs. Vernon very nervous, and for two nights the lady slept but little.

Robert noticed the change in her condition, and pitied her greatly.

"It's a shame that Frederic Vernon can't turn over a new leaf," he thought. "But I am afraid that it isn't in him."

On the day that Mrs. Vernon expected a reply to her cablegram she felt worse than ever, and Robert suggested that they take a drive together.

"We can go along the river road, and then along the cliffs," he said. "I am certain the morning air will do you good, for it promises to be very clear."

"Very well, Robert. I will go with you, and you can get a team without delay," she answered.

"And shall I drive?"

"If you want to."

Mrs. Vernon spoke thus, for Robert had taken her out a number of times and had always proved a very careful and reliable driver.

In a few minutes Robert was on his way to the livery stable. He met Frederic Vernon on the street, bound for his aunt's boarding place.

"Hullo, Frost, how is my aunt to-day?" cried the young man.

"Not so well, Mr. Vernon."

"That's too bad. What seems to be the trouble?"

"She can't sleep nights, so she says."

As Robert spoke he looked sharply at the fellow, but Vernon did not change color.

"You ought to take her out for a drive," said the young man.

"That is just what I am going to do."

"Indeed! This morning?"

"Yes, just as soon as I can get a team and a carriage."

"Good for you. I would take her out myself but somehow I never made a fist at driving."

"That is strange. I thought all young men in your station of life liked to drive."

"Well--er--the trouble is, I was scared by a horse when I was a little boy. I've never liked horseflesh since."

"I see. Well, I have never yet seen the team I was afraid of," answered Robert, telling the exact truth.

"Is that so? Well, your time may come."

There was a significance in Frederic Vernon's words which was lost upon our hero.

"Where are you going to drive?" went on the spendthrift.

"Along the river road first, and then along the cliffs."

And with these words Robert passed on. He was afraid that if he stopped to talk longer Frederic Vernon might invite himself to go along, and he was quite certain the ride would do Mrs. Vernon no good were such the case.

Watching his opportunity, Vernon followed our hero and saw Robert hire a team of white and gray horses, and have them hooked up to a light road carriage.

Then he hurried to his boarding house with a peculiar smile on his evil face.

"I can see that team coming a long way off," he said to himself. "And I won't make any mistake."

With quite a little flourish Robert drove around to Mrs. Cabe's boarding place, and tied up at the block. Soon Mrs. Vernon came out, and he handed her to a seat.

"I met your nephew when I went to the livery stable," he observed, as he drove away. "Did he come in?"

"No," answered Mrs. Vernon. "Where was he going?"

"I thought he was coming to see you."

"Did he want to know if I was going out?"

"He suggested I take you for a drive, after I told him you were not very well again."

"I wonder he never offers to take me driving," mused the lady.

"He said he didn't like to drive--that he was afraid of horses."

"What, Frederic? Why, he used to own a very fast horse and go out driving in Lincoln Park at home nearly every day."

"He told me he had been frightened when a boy by a horse, and had never cared for horseflesh since."

"That is not true, Robert. How queer that he should tell such a falsehood. Do you suppose he did it just to get out of driving me?"

"I don't know what to think, Mrs. Vernon. On the whole, I think your nephew is a very peculiar young man."

"It's too bad." Mrs. Vernon gave a deep sigh. "And he is the only near relative I have!"

Fearful that the drive would do the lady small good if they continued to talk about Frederic Vernon, Robert changed the subject, and so skillfully did he manage it that presently Mrs. Vernon grew quite cheerful. Down along the river they stopped for a few minutes, and the boy picked a bunch of wild flowers and presented them to his companion.

At length they left the river road and took to that running up along the cliffs previously mentioned. This road was but little used, but its wildness was attractive to both Mrs. Vernon and the youth, for from the upper heights they could see for many miles around.

"I would not mind owning a summer home up here," said Mrs. Vernon, as they halted at the highest point in the road. "See how beautiful the Thames looks, winding along through the meadows and woods below us."

"It is nice," answered Robert. "But as for a summer home, I rather think I would prefer one in the United States."

The lady smiled.

"I can see you are an out-and-out Yankee lad, Robert. Well, I cannot blame you. I agree that our life at home is good enough for anybody."

Presently Robert started the team again, and they bowled along the edge of the cliff at a rapid gait.

To one side was a mass of rocks and shrubbery, while to the other was a valley or gorge forty or fifty feet deep, at the bottom of which flowed a tiny brook on its way to the River Thames.

The team was a fresh one, and the drive along the river had just warmed them up. They went along at a spanking pace, and Robert had his hands full holding them in. But it was a pleasant task.

"I love a good team," he said, as they sped along. "No old slow-pokes for me."

"You are certain you can control them?" asked Mrs. Vernon, as the horses stepped out livelier than ever.

"Oh, yes, they are all right," he answered.

A quarter of a mile more was covered, when they reached a point where the cliff road wound around a sharp bend.

Mrs. Vernon had just called Robert's attention to a pretty scene in the valley far below, when of a sudden somebody leaped out in the road in front of the horses.

It was a man wrapped in a white sheet and with a pistol in his hand.

The pistol was discharged, and one end of the sheet waved wildly at the same time.

The mettlesome horses were badly frightened and reared and plunged wildly.

"Oh, Robert, we will be killed!" burst from Mrs. Vernon's lips. "We will be thrown over the cliff!"

"Don't jump!" he answered, as he saw her rise up as if to leap from the carriage.

He held the reins tightly and spoke to the team as gently as possible. But now another pistol shot rang out, and off sped the team on a furious gallop down the cliff road, with the carriage bumping and rocking after them.

Robert felt that a crisis in his life had suddenly arisen. Should he lose all control of the horses it was more than likely that they would leap over the cliff, and that would mean death for both Mrs. Vernon and himself. All in a flash it came to him that Frederic Vernon must have been the man wound in the white sheet who had fired the pistol.

"The scoundrel!" he thought. "If we get out of this alive, he'll have a big score to settle with me!"

On and on plunged the team, the carriage jolting from side to side, and Mrs. Vernon prepared to leap out at the first move the horses might make toward the gorge. Robert held on to the lines like grim death, his feet braced firmly against the dashboard. It was truly a ride for life or death. In the meantime the man in the white sheet had disappeared as suddenly as he had come.

So far the road had been tolerably even, but now came a stretch which was rough, and the carriage came closer and closer to the edge of the cliff.

"We are going!" shrieked Mrs. Vernon.

"Not yet," answered Robert, and tried to pull the team around. He had partly succeeded when snap! went one of the reins, and he was thrown backward.

The breaking of the rein presented a new obstacle to be overcome, and for the second our hero did not know what to do. The team were now out of control, and even the youth was afraid they might leap over the cliff at any instant.

But then a new thought occurred to him, and as quick as a flash he stood up and leaped to the back of one of the horses.

"Whoa!" he shouted. "Whoa!" and clapped his hat over the creature's eyes.

A rearing and a plunging followed. But the horse slowed up and brought the carriage around to the thicket opposite to the cliff. A crashing of bushes followed, and in a few seconds more the team was halted. One of the wheels of the carriage was badly shattered and one horse was cut about the legs, but otherwise no damage was done.

CHAPTER XXI.
THE CABLEGRAM FROM CHICAGO.

As soon as the team came to a halt Robert leaped to the ground and held their heads.

"Now you can get out, Mrs. Vernon," he said.

"Thank God we are safe!" murmured the lady.

She was so weak she could scarcely stand, and once having left the carriage she sank down on a flat rock, her breast heaving with emotion.

Robert tied the team fast to a nearby tree, and then came to her side.

"You are not hurt, are you?" he asked anxiously.

"I--I believe not," she faltered. "But, oh, Robert, we had a very narrow escape!"

"That is so, Mrs. Vernon."

"Had the carriage gone over the cliff nothing could have saved us from death!"

"Yes, it would have been a nasty fall."

"And that man who scared the team----" She paused. "Do you imagine----" She could go no further.

"Let us talk about that later on, Mrs. Vernon," he put in hastily. "You had better rest here while I see how much the carriage is damaged."

Our hero made the examination, and speedily found that the wheel was too badly shattered to permit the turnout being used again until it was repaired.

"I'll have to get another carriage," he said. "What will you do, remain here until I get back?"

"No! no!" she cried. "I--I--that man--he may come again----" She gazed at him with a world of meaning in her eyes.

"You are right," answered Robert. "There is a cottage some distance down the road. Can you walk that far with me?"

Mrs. Vernon said she would try, and they started out. As they approached the cottage they met the owner coming away in his wagon.

Matters were quickly explained to the Englishman, and he readily agreed to drive them both back to the village.

"I hav'n't no quick horses for to run away with ye!" he grinned. "But I can git ye there in time an' safe, too."

They seated themselves on a back seat of the farm wagon, and started. The pace was a slow one, and it was fully an hour before they reached the village and the turnout came to a halt before Mrs. Cabe's door.

"Let the livery stable people attend to the wreck," said Mrs. Vernon, "and tell them to send the bill to me."

"And what of the man who scared us?" asked Robert. "Shall I put the constable on his track?"

Mrs. Vernon's face became a study.

"Robert, what do you think of this?"

"What do you mean?"

"Have you any idea who it was?"

"Frankly, I have, Mrs. Vernon."

"You imagine it was Frederic?"

"I do."

"But why should he want to--to----" She could get no further, but burst into tears.

"Don't you remember he wanted to know about your will? He has probably found out that you have not yet altered it, and----"

"Well?"

"Well, he wanted to get you out of the way before any change was made. I am sorry to speak so plainly, but I think your nephew is a thorough villain."

"But we may be mistaken. The man may have been an ordinary highwayman."

Robert shook his head. "I don't believe there are highwaymen in this part of England."

Satisfied that the lady would be safe for the time being, Robert hurried off to the livery stable and explained matters to the proprietor.

"The horses got frightened on the road," he said, "and in saving them from going over the cliff I had to turn them into a thicket. A wheel is broken and one horse has his legs scratched."

"And who is going to foot the bill?" growled the livery stable keeper, imagining he scented trouble.

"Mrs. Vernon will pay any fair bill you may present. But she will pay no fancy price for the damage done."

"Oh, all right, I won't charge her any more than is necessary," said the man, much relieved.

He wished to know how the team had become frightened, but Robert evaded the question, for Mrs. Vernon had not given him permission to speak of the matter. Evidently the lady wished to think over it before deciding what to do.

When the young secretary returned to the boarding house he found Mrs. Vernon lying down, having taken a quieting draught. He attended to the writing of several letters, and was just finishing up when a messenger appeared from the telegraph office.

"The cablegram," said Robert, looking at the envelope.

"Read it, Robert," said the lady, and opening the communication he did as requested. The cablegram was from Mr. Farley. It read as follows:

"Check 865, Frederic Vernon. Six hundred dollars."

"Check number 865," murmured Mrs. Vernon. "Robert, what is the last stub number in my book?"

"Number 838."

"Then check number 865 is a forgery!"

The young secretary bowed.

"It was drawn to the order of Frederic Vernon, and probably cashed by him," went on the lady, her breath coming short and fast.

"Mrs. Vernon, we are only reaching a conclusion we guessed at long ago," said the youth soothingly.

"I know, I know, Robert! Yet I had hoped there might be some mistake!"

"Your nephew is unworthy of the interest you take in him."

"That is where he got his money to come here."

"He was a fool to commit the forgery. He must have known that it would be discovered sooner or later," said Robert bluntly. He felt that the sooner Mrs. Vernon realized the utter rascality of her nephew the better it would be for the lady.

"But if I had been killed--if both of us had been killed----" she began.

"Then the forgery would never have been discovered, for your nephew would have taken charge of everything, including your private papers and your check-books."

"It is terrible! terrible!" The lady buried her face in a sofa pillow and began to weep. "Robert, what would you advise me to do?" she asked, after a while.

"Do you want my candid opinion?" he questioned.

"I do."

"I would have a straight talk with your nephew, and then send him about his business, and tell him if he ever came near me again I would have him arrested."

"I cannot be so harsh with one of my own flesh and blood."

"Well, then, I tell you what you might do. You might give him, say, a thousand dollars, with the understanding that he leave the country, and that he does not go back to the United States."

"But where would he go?"

"There are lots of places to go to--South Africa, South America, or Australia. With a thousand dollars and his passage money he might set himself up in some sort of business and get rich."

Mrs. Vernon's face brightened.

"If he would only do that I might be so glad! If he really made a man of himself I would not cut him out of my will."

"I would not allow him to be around where I was. He is too dangerous a young man. He may try to poison you next."

Mrs. Vernon shivered.

"Yes, and he may try poisoning you, too, Robert," she said. "I must be very careful. It would not be right for me to let you run any more risk. Perhaps you would prefer to leave my services."

"Mrs. Vernon, I will never leave you--at least, so long as you wish me to stay," he cried impulsively.

"You are a true friend, Robert, and I should not like to part with you. I will have a talk with Frederic as soon as he shows himself."

"I would like to be present at the interview, Mrs. Vernon."

"Yes?"

"I want to make certain that he tries no violence. After this I am going to arm myself with a pistol," added Robert.

"You shall be present, Robert. But perhaps Frederic will not come again--if he imagines that we suspect him."

"He will hang around as long as he dares. He can get hold of no money excepting what he wrings from you, and he knows it."

At that moment a servant knocked on the door.

"What is wanted?" asked our hero, who went to answer the summons.

"Mr. Parsons come to see you and Mrs. Vernon," answered the girl.

"Mr. Parsons?" repeated the young secretary. "Who is he?"

"A farmer, please sir, as lives up back of the cliff. He says he saw you driving, and he has something to tell you."

"He must know something of importance," put in Mrs. Vernon eagerly. "Show him up, Lucy."

In a moment more Farmer Parsons, a short, ruddy-faced Englishman, entered the apartment hat in hand. Robert gave him a chair, and then closed the door tightly, that no outsiders might hear what the newcomer had to tell.

CHAPTER XXII.
FARMER PARSONS' STORY.

"You will excuse me for troubling you," began Farmer Parsons, after bowing several times to Mrs. Vernon and Robert. "But I thought I just had to come in and tell you that I couldn't help a-doing of it."

"Couldn't help doing what?" questioned Mrs. Vernon, in perplexity.

"Giving him a sound trouncing, lady. I thought as how he deserved it, I did."

"Whom did you whip?" asked Robert.

"Why, the lady's relative, of course!" cried the farmer, in surprise. "Isn't he back yet?"

"No, we have seen nothing of him."

Farmer Parsons fell back in his chair in open-mouthed surprise.

"By Harry! then I suppose I've put my foot into it!" he gasped.

"Into what?" asked Robert, although he guessed at the truth.

"Why I--that is--you see I collared him on the road and I couldn't help but give him the worst trouncing I guess he ever got in his life. He threatened to have me locked up, so I thought I would come here and explain matters."

"You caught Frederic Vernon up on the cliff road?" asked Mrs. Vernon.

"I did, madam--jest after he had up and scared your horses so that they ran away."

"Then it was Frederic, beyond a doubt," murmured the lady faintly.

"He said as how he had done it only in fun," went on the English farmer. "But I said it was mighty poor fun, and he deserved a thrashing."

"And then you whipped him?" said Robert.

"No, I didn't trounce him until after he got impudent and told me to shut up and mind my own affairs. I told him he might have killed both on you."

"And what did he say to that?" asked our hero curiously.

"He said he knew what he was doing and I must keep my mouth shut, or he would lay the whole thing off on to me. Then I up and knocked him down, madam, and when he comes back it will be limping and with a black eye. But I don't care," added the farmer defiantly. "He deserved it."

"I do not blame you, Mr. Parsons," said Mrs. Vernon quietly. "It was a--a mean thing for him to do."

"Some folks would have him arrested for it, madam."

"I do not doubt but that they would. Where did you leave my nephew?"

"I left him to find his way back to the village the best he could. But before we parted I took this thing away from him. I was afraid if I didn't he might shoot me."

Farmer Parsons reached into one of the deep pockets of his coat and brought forth a nickel-plated revolver.

Mrs. Vernon received it gingerly and passed it over to Robert.

"Is it empty?" she asked.

"No, it has two cartridges still in it," answered the young secretary, after an examination.

"I do not know what to do with it, Robert. I do not want it."

"I reckon I'll keep it for the present, Mrs. Vernon," said our hero, and placed the pistol in his hip pocket.

The lady turned to Farmer Parsons.

"I do not blame you for what you have done," she said. "I imagine my nephew got what he deserved. But I hate a family scandal, and I wish you would not say anything about this matter unless I call upon you."

"As you will, madam; only I don't want no trouble----"

"You shall get into no trouble, Mr. Parsons; I will see to that. And for coming here, I will pay you for your time."

Farmer Parsons wished to refuse, but he was a poor man with a large family to support and he readily accepted the two pounds--about ten dollars--which Mrs. Vernon tendered him.

"Very much obliged, madam," he said, as he bowed himself out. "But take my advice and watch your nevvy--watch him closely, for he's a bad un, he is!" And in a moment he was lumbering down the stairs again.

For several minutes after the farmer was gone Mrs. Vernon said nothing. She began to pace the floor nervously. The last of her faith in her graceless nephew was shattered.

"He is a villain, Robert," she said at last. "A villain in every sense of the word. There does not seem to be a redeeming trait in his whole character."

"Well, I wouldn't say that exactly, Mrs. Vernon. But one thing is certain, he is too dangerous a character to be allowed to remain where you are."

"You are right, and I shall send him off as you suggested."

"And if he won't go?"

"He will go--or else he shall go to jail."

For once Mrs. Vernon spoke firmly and in a manner that admitted of no dispute. It took a long time to arouse her, but once aroused her nature was a thoroughly stubborn one.

In the meantime Frederic Vernon had found his way to one of the ale-houses of the village. As Farmer Parsons had said, he had suffered a severe chastisement and he could scarcely walk. His chin and one eye were much swollen, and his back felt as if it had been pounded into a jelly.

"I'll get even with that man," he muttered. "I'd give a hundred dollars to see him hanged!"

Entering the ale-house he called for a glass of liquor, and then explained that he had suffered a severe fall from the cliff. As he had spent considerable money in the resort the landlord was all attention and led him to a side room, where he was given the chance to brush and wash up. At the same time the landlord's wife sewed up several rents in his coat and gave him a bit of court-plaster for a cut on his hand.

It must be confessed that Frederic Vernon was in a most unsettled state of mind. He hardly knew whether he dared to go to his aunt or not. From the landlord of the ale-house he learned that both Mrs. Vernon and Robert had escaped without serious physical injury, although the report was around that the lady was suffering from severe shock.

"I must put on a bold front," he told himself at last. "After all, my word is as good as that yokel's."

To put on a bold front, as he expressed it, Frederic Vernon drank rather more than was good for him, and then with a swagger he made his way to Mrs. Cabe's house that evening after supper.

"I want to see my aunt," he said to the landlady.

"Mrs. Vernon is not feeling very well," said Mrs. Cabe.

"I guess she will see me," he returned, and pushed past her and up to Mrs. Vernon's apartment. Robert heard him coming, and the two met at the door.

"What do you want?" asked our hero shortly. He saw at once that Vernon was partly under the influence of liquor.

"None of your business," retorted the young man. "My business is with my aunt."

"She is not well to-night."

"Then it is your fault, Frost. I heard all about how you let those horses run away with her."

By this time Mrs. Vernon had come to the door, and Frederic Vernon pushed his way into the room. Robert followed, and at the same time his hand went into his pocket to feel if the pistol Farmer Parsons had surrendered was still where he had placed it.

"Well, aunt, I've heard that you came close to losing your life this noon," began Frederic Vernon.

"It is true," answered Mrs. Vernon coldly.

"You ought not to let that boy drive you out. He might have lost all control and you would have been killed."

"It was not Robert's fault that the horses ran away."

"They wouldn't have run away had I been driving them."

"Frederic, I think it is about time that this farce came to an end. You know well enough what made our team run away in the first place."

The young man drew back.

"Why--er----" he stammered.

"You scared them with your white sheet and the pistol."

"It's false, aunt. Was that yokel of an Englishman here with his lying story?"

"Mr. Parsons was here, yes, and he told the truth, Frederic. You are an out-and-out rascal. My eyes are open at last, and you shall no longer deceive me."

As Mrs. Vernon spoke she faced the young man so sternly that he felt compelled to fall back, while his eyes sought the floor.

"I--I never deceived you, aunt."

"You have deceived me from start to finish, Frederic. At first you neglected my business and caused me several heavy losses. Then, when I engaged Robert to take your place, you tried to get him into trouble over my jewelry. After that you hired that Dr. Remington to aid you in placing me in an insane asylum, and your plot might have proved a success had I not left America. After that, running short of money, you forged my name to a check for six hundred dollars. And now you have finished up by trying to kill both Robert and me. Frederic, I am done with you, and I never want you to come near me again."

As Mrs. Vernon concluded the tears started down her cheeks, and she turned away to hide her emotions. Utterly dumfounded, Frederic Vernon sank in an easy chair the picture of despair. He realized that complete exposure had come at last, and he wondered what his rich relative would do with him.

CHAPTER XXIII.
AUNT AND NEPHEW'S AGREEMENT.

"Aunt, you don't mean it!" gasped Frederic Vernon, when he felt able to speak.

"I do mean it, Frederic, and it will be useless for you to argue the question," replied the lady, firmly.

"But this is a--a--all a mistake," he faltered.

"There is no mistake. And as I just said, I will not argue the question."

"You--you cast me out?"

"I do."

"But if you do that, what shall I do?"

"Go to work and make a man of yourself. Do that, and perhaps in time I will do something for you."

Frederic Vernon shook his head slowly. Then he faced Robert, and his proud face became black with illy-suppressed rage.

"This is your work, you young rascal----" he began, when his aunt stopped him.

"I will hear no talk like that here, Frederic," she said. "Robert is my best and truest friend, and you must respect him as such."

"He has done everything he could to cut me out!" howled the young spendthrift bitterly.

"That ain't so," burst out Robert. "You cut yourself out. Your aunt would never have discharged you had you done your work properly--she has told me that a number of times."

"I say it's a plot against me!" said Frederic Vernon, hardly knowing how to go on.

"Frederic, you are a very foolish young man," came from Mrs. Vernon gravely. "There was a time when I had unlimited confidence in you, and you could have retained that confidence had you chosen so to do. Instead, you became a spendthrift. Now you must go out into the world and earn your own living."

"What am I to go at?" he asked, in a hopeless tone. For the time being he seemed utterly crushed.

"You have a fair commercial education. You might become a bookkeeper."

"Bookkeepers don't earn their salt!" he snapped.

"Some of them earn twenty to forty dollars per week," put in Robert.

"Twenty to forty dollars! Do you suppose I am going to live on a beggarly twenty dollars per week! Perhaps a low-bred boy like you can do it. I am used to something better."

"I am not a low-bred boy," retorted Robert, clenching his fists, at which Frederic Vernon fell back before him. "I consider my breeding as good as yours, perhaps better."

"I will have no further arguments or quarrels," said Mrs. Vernon, coming between them.

"Aunt, do you mean to throw me off without a cent?" pleaded Frederic Vernon. "If you do that I shall starve, here among strangers. At least, pay my fare back to the United States."

"I do not want you to go back to the United States."

"Then where shall I go?"

"I have been thinking that over. Your best plan will be to strike out for some new country, say South Africa, South America, or perhaps Australia, where you can take a fresh start in life."

"I can't go to any of those places without money."

"I understand there are splendid openings in South Africa, and in Australia. If you will agree to go to one or the other of those places, and to keep away from the United States for at least five years, I will pay your passage money and give you a thousand dollars besides."

The young man's face brightened, but then it fell again.

"A thousand dollars isn't much," he ventured.

"It is enough."

"Make it five thousand, aunt, and I'll agree never to bother you again."

"No, I will not give you a cent more than the thousand dollars, and Robert shall buy your passage ticket."

"Always that boy!" howled the young man. "Cannot you trust me even to buy my own ticket?"

"I am sorry to say I cannot."

"You won't make it two thousand?" pleaded the wayward nephew.

"Well, I will give you fifteen hundred dollars," replied Mrs. Vernon, weakening a little. "That will give you a splendid start in some new place. Some men have made fortunes in South Africa and in Australia."

"I don't want to go to South Africa; I might try Australia. Dick Roberts went to Sydney, and, I believe, is doing first-rate."

"You ought to do as well as young Roberts. You have just as good an education."

"And how soon do you want me to start?"

"You must start within the next week."

"That is rather short notice."

"There is nothing to keep you here. You can find out when the Australian steamer leaves, and what the fare is, to-morrow," replied Mrs. Vernon.

A long discussion followed, in which Robert took but small part. In vain Frederic Vernon pleaded for more money and more time. Mrs. Vernon remained obdurate, and at last the graceless nephew bid her good-night and left. As the door closed after him the lady uttered a heavy sigh of relief.

"I am glad that is over, Robert," she murmured.

"It was certainly a heavy trial for you," he said, with a smile of sympathy.

"I trust he doesn't bother me any more before he leaves."

"I think it won't do any harm if I watch him and see what moves he makes. He may try to play some game upon you at the last minute, you know."

"Perhaps you are right, Robert. But so long as he remains around I shall try to look out for myself."

The next morning Robert met Frederic Vernon on the street, near the post-office.

At once the spendthrift caught our hero by the arm.

"Come along, I want to talk to you," he said, with a dark look on his face.

Feeling well able to take care of himself, Robert followed the young man down a side street which was practically deserted.

"You think you are mighty smart, don't you?" began Vernon, as soon as he felt that they were out of hearing of outsiders.

"I think I am smart in some things, Mr. Vernon," replied Robert, as coolly as he could.

"You think it's a fine thing to have me shipped off to Australia."

"It may prove the making of you."

"You want to get me out of the way so that you can get hold of my aunt's fortune."

"Well, it will be a good thing for her and for me when you are out of the way. You are too dangerous a young man to have around."

"Bah! What I have done against her doesn't amount to shucks."

"There is a difference of opinion on that score."

Frederic Vernon shook his fist in Robert's face.

"You have me down now, and I can't help myself," he hissed. "But my time will come, remember that!"

"Are you going to Australia, as your aunt wishes?"

"That is none of your business."

"She has made it my business."

"Do you mean to say you have been sent to watch me?"

"Yes, I am going to see that you are going to leave England, as intended."

"Then that is another score I will have to settle with you."

Without a word more, Frederic Vernon turned on his heel and hurried away.

Robert continued to the post-office for the mail, and then purchased a railroad and steamship guide.

In the guide he found that a steamer for Australia would sail from Liverpool on the next Tuesday at noon. He also learned where tickets could be procured, and the rate of fare.

With this information he returned to Mrs. Vernon.

One of the letters from America interested the lady deeply.

"I ought to return to Chicago at once," she said, after reading it. "There is to be a change in a manufacturing company in which I hold a large interest."

"Well, your nephew can sail for Australia on Tuesday," answered Robert. "We might return to New York by steamer, starting a day or two later."

That afternoon Frederic Vernon called upon his aunt again. He was quite humble now, for the last of the six hundred dollars procured on the forged check had been spent, and he was afraid Mrs. Vernon might cut him off entirely unless he agreed to do exactly as she desired.

"Robert tells me there is a steamer for Australia on Tuesday next," said the lady. "You can take that, Frederic."

"Very well," he answered. "But I must have the money for the ticket. I am dead broke."

"I will give you five pounds to spend on an outfit and to keep you until you sail. Robert will buy your ticket."

"I am old enough to do that myself," grumbled Frederic.

"No; I prefer to have him do so," said Mrs. Vernon pointedly, and the nephew did not dare to argue the point.

The ticket was bought on Saturday. Then Mrs. Vernon announced that Robert should see the young man to Liverpool and to the steamer.

"I hope all goes well," said Mrs. Vernon to our hero in private. "You must make certain that Frederic sails as intended."

CHAPTER XXIV.
THE ATTACK IN THE STATEROOM.

Frederic Vernon was only calm outwardly; inwardly he was boiling with rage, and more than anxious to "get square" with Robert.

He attributed his downfall completely to the young secretary.

"If it hadn't been for him I could have hoodwinked aunt right along," he told himself. "It's a shame that I've got to do just what that boy wants me to."

As soon as he heard that Robert was going to accompany him to Liverpool, he set to work to hatch up some plot against our hero.

Robert was to carry the fifteen hundred dollars, and give it to Frederic when the time came for the steamer to depart, and when young Vernon was on board.

Frederic Vernon spent Sunday night with his aunt, and did what he could to get Mrs. Vernon to allow him a little more money. As a consequence, he came away a hundred dollars richer than would otherwise have been the case.

Nor was this all. At the last minute, while the aunt was getting the money for him, he picked up some of Mrs. Vernon's jewels and slipped them into his pocket. Among the jewels was a diamond crescent worth five hundred dollars, and a pair of earrings worth three hundred dollars more.

Mrs. Vernon was not feeling well, and as soon as her nephew left she retired for the night, and the jewels were not missed until forty-eight hours later.

Early the next morning Frederic Vernon started for Liverpool, with Robert with him.

"I won't wake my aunt up to say good-by," said the young man. "I always hate a scene."

"She will be glad not to be disturbed," thought Robert, but said nothing.

Arriving in Liverpool Frederic Vernon set about buying such things as he thought he would need on his long ocean trip.

"Will you go along to the shops?" he asked Robert.

"No, I will remain at the hotel," answered our hero.

So Frederic Vernon went off alone. He had no heart to buy what was needed, for the thought of going to Australia was very distasteful to him.

"It won't be like living in Chicago or New York," he thought. "It's beastly uncivilized out there. I wish I could put Frost in my place and stay behind myself."

Among the places he visited was a ticket broker's office, and here he asked what they would give for the ticket to Australia.

Tickets were just then in good demand, and the broker looked the matter up.

"I'll give you seventy-five per cent. of its cost," he said. "But I want the ticket right away."

"I can give it to you in about an hour."

"That is positive?"

"Yes."

"Very well, bring it to me. I have a customer who wishes just such a ticket, but I cannot hold him long."

At once Frederic hurried back to the hotel.

"I am going on board the steamer at once," he said. "Give me my ticket."

"You seem to be in a tremendous hurry," said Robert suspiciously.

"Well, I'll tell you the truth, Frost, since we are to part to meet no more. Some of my old creditors are after me and I want to give them the slip."

"I see."

Robert felt it would not be honorable to help Frederic Vernon escape his creditors, but at the same time there was no use in detaining the young man, since he would have no money with which to settle his old obligations.

But he would not give up the ticket.

"I will go to the steamer with you, and give you the ticket there," he said.

He was firm in this, and wondering what he had best do next, Frederic Vernon led the way to the street and hailed a passing cab.

The two got in and were driven to the docks without delay. The young man had his hand-baggage with him.

"Now I am off," he said. "Give me the ticket and the money, and good-by to you."

"I will take you on the steamer," said Robert firmly.

Vernon grated his teeth, but had to agree, and both went on board, and down to the stateroom which had been selected. It was a room for two, but as yet Vernon occupied it alone.

"Now let me see that money and the ticket," snapped the young man. "I am not going off until I am sure that everything is right."

Sitting down on the edge of the lower berth, Robert brought out the articles in question, and passed them over. Vernon inspected the ticket closely and counted the money.

"There is twenty dollars missing," he declared.

"No, the money is all right," cried Robert.

"Well, count it out to me and see for yourself."

Anxious to prove that the amount was correct Robert began to count the bills one after another.

As he was doing this Frederic Vernon suddenly raised the umbrella he carried and brought down the heavy handle with crushing force on the boy's head.

The blow was as cruel as it was unexpected, and with a groan Robert fell forward on the stateroom floor.

Vernon bent over him, to find that he was totally unconscious, and liable to remain so for some time to come.

"That's the time I paid him off," muttered the rascal. "I'll teach him to meddle in my private affairs."

He gathered up the ticket and the money, and prepared to leave the stateroom. Then a sickly smile came over his face.

"Might as well be hung for a sheep as a lamb," he muttered, and going back he relieved Robert of his watch, his pocketbook, and the scarfpin Mrs. Vernon had given him.

"I reckon I'll be pretty well fixed for awhile," said the young rascal to himself. "And if the steamer carries him off to South Africa or Australia perhaps I'll be able to tell aunt a pretty good story and get back into her good graces."

Leaving the stateroom he locked the door, and as an extra precaution he stuffed the keyhole with a paper wad.

"Now he won't get out in a hurry, even if he does come around," he added, and hurried on deck and to the crowded dock. Soon he was lost to view amid the people and drays that were coming and going.

Half an hour after Frederic Vernon's departure a burly man of forty-five came on board the steamer and engaged the vacant berth in the stateroom Robert was occupying.

"I hope I have a good room-mate," observed Mr. Pelham, as he found his way below. "Frederic Vernon, eh? Well, that's a pretty good name."

He reached the stateroom, and finding the door locked, knocked upon it several times.

No answer came back, and Mr. Pelham was perplexed.

"Can the key be at the office?" he mused, and went off to see if such was the case.

Of course the article was not there, and a porter followed him to the room to let him in.

"The keyhole is stuffed," said the porter, after an examination. "Some of the children on board have been playing pranks again."

"Hark!" cried Mr. Pelham. "Am I mistaken, or did I hear a groan?"

He and the porter listened. The gentleman was not mistaken, for now a second groan sounded out, more loudly than the first.

"Your room-mate must be sick!" cried the porter. "Hi, there, sir, please open the door?" he called.

But Robert paid no attention, for he was not yet conscious. The porter dug away at the paper wad, and at last extricated it from the keyhole. Then he inserted the key and swung the door back.

Both men uttered exclamations of horror, for Robert lay across the lower berth unconscious, and with a small stream of blood running over his temple and cheek.

"Gracious! This looks like suicide!" ejaculated Mr. Pelham. "Run for the captain and a doctor, quick!"

The porter needed no second bidding, and made off with all speed. When he returned he found that Mr. Pelham had propped Robert up on a pillow and bound up the small wound on our hero's head with a handkerchief.

"Whe--where is he?" were Robert's first words.

"He? Who?" asked the men who surrounded him.

"Frederic Vernon, the man who struck me down."

"So you were struck down?" said the captain of the steamer.

"I--I was," gasped Robert. "Did he--he escape?"

The others looked around, but of course Vernon was nowhere to be seen.

"He must have escaped," said Mr. Pelham. "Frederic Vernon, you said. He was to be my room-mate."

A number of questions followed, and Robert told his tale, to which the others listened with close attention. Then a search was instituted for Frederic Vernon, but this was unsuccessful.

"He has left the ship," declared the captain. "It's not likely that he wanted to go to Australia."

It was not until some time later that Robert discovered the loss of his purse, watch, and the scarfpin, and then he was more angry than ever.

"Oh, if only I can lay hands on him," he thought. "I'll make him suffer for all his evil doings!"

CHAPTER XXV.
A FRIEND IN NEED.

The steamer was now ready to sail, and Robert went ashore with a number of others who had come aboard to see their friends off.

Just as he left the gang-plank a belated passenger came rushing on the ship. It was the man who purchased Frederic Vernon's ticket at the cut-rate office.

It must be confessed that Robert was much downcast as he walked slowly away from the dock. Here he was in Liverpool without a shilling in his pocket, and the mission he had undertaken for Mrs. Vernon had proved a miserable failure.

"I was a chump not to watch Vernon more closely," he muttered to himself. "I might have known that he was just waiting to get the best of me."

Presently the idea struck him that Frederic Vernon might be watching the steamer to learn whether or not his victim would come ashore or set sail in the ship.

"I'll see if he is anywhere around," he thought, and set out on the hunt without delay.

The docks were piled high with merchandise of all sorts, and thus afforded numerous hiding places.

Robert made his way from one corner to another, until he reached a tall pile of lumber. On the top of this were seated half a dozen boys and a young man.

The latter individual was Frederic Vernon, who had returned to the dock to do just as our hero had suspected.

Vernon saw Robert at the same instant that the boy spotted him, and before our hero could reach the place he leaped from the lumber pile and started on a dead run for the street beyond the dock.

"Hi, stop!" cried Robert, giving chase. "Stop the thief!"

The boys and a number of others took up the cry, and in a few minutes fully a score of people were following Frederic Vernon.

Down one street and up another went the crowd, Vernon keeping fully a square ahead of them. Robert was nearest to him, and presently saw the rascal dart into an alleyway. When our hero reached the alleyway Vernon was out of sight.

Robert and the crowd searched the alleyway from end to end, but without success. Vernon had slipped all of his pursuers, and had hired a cab to take him to another part of the city.

The rascal remained in hiding at an obscure boarding house for nearly a week, and then took passage for Boston, satisfied that since Robert had not sailed for Australia, it would be worse than useless for him to appeal again to his aunt.

After the chase was over Robert found himself tired out and as hungry as a bear. Moreover his head, which the ship's doctor had patched up with court-plaster, hurt him not a little.

"Another failure," he muttered disconsolately. "Did ever a fellow have such a run of bad luck before!"

Had Vernon not been a close relative of the lady who employed him, Robert would have put the case in the hands of the Liverpool police, and got them to telegraph to Mrs. Vernon for him for aid. But this he knew would not suit the lady at all.

"I must find some means of getting back to Chishing without the aid of the police," he told himself. "Perhaps I'll run across somebody I know."

He scanned every face he met, but for several hours was unsuccessful. At last he met a farmer he had seen on the River Thames several times. Farmer Goodall had come to Liverpool to see his son off, who was bound for America. Father and son had just separated when our hero ran across the former.

"How do you do, Mr. Goodall," said Robert, extending his hand. "I trust you remember me."

"Indeed I do, Mr. Frost," answered the farmer, as he shook hands. "What brings you here? Are you going back home?"

"Not yet. I came on a little business for Mrs. Vernon. You know I am her private secretary."

"So they told me in the village, sir."

"I was just looking for somebody I might know," went on the youth. "I've got myself into trouble."

"Indeed, and how is that?"

"I've been robbed of my watch, my scarfpin and my money."

"Gracious me! is it possible, Mr. Frost? It must have been a bold thief that could do that."

"He caught me in an out-of-the-way spot and hit me over the head." Robert showed the plastered cut. "I just wish I could get hold of him."

"I've no doubt of that, sir. So he stole your pocketbook, eh? Then perhaps you are out of money."

"I am, and I was just looking for somebody who would advance me enough with which to get my dinner and a railway ticket to Chishing. Of course as soon as I get back Mrs. Vernon will, I am certain, make good the amount."

"Then in that case I'll advance what you need," answered Farmer Goodall. "But I am going back myself, and perhaps we can travel together, if you don't mind."

"Not at all."

"I generally travel second-class, but if you----"

"Second class will suit me well enough, Mr. Goodall. In America, you know, we have no classes at all, although in the South we have coaches for white folks, and coaches--we call them cars--for colored people."

"So I've heard. I suppose my son John will see many strange sights when he gets to New York. I've just been seeing him off."

"He will, for New York is somewhat different from any city you have over here. Is he going to remain in New York?"

"No, he's going to Chicago first, and then to what they call the West. I don't know much about it, but I hope the buffaloes and Indians don't kill him, that's all. Come on and have something to eat."

"I don't believe the buffaloes and Indians will trouble him," said Robert, as they moved toward an eating house. "There are very few buffaloes left, and none around the cities and towns, and as for the Indians they are quite peaceful now and live on the reservations the government has allotted them."

"It must be a great country. I wanted to go there when I was a young man, but my wife objected. She didn't want to take the long voyage over the ocean."

"That I presume was before we had the swift ocean steamers."

"Yes. Those that went over took the sailing vessels, and the trip lasted about a couple of months or so."

They entered a modest but respectable eating house, and here Farmer Goodall ordered a substantial dinner for two. He looked curiously at Robert when the youth turned down his glass.

"What, lad, won't have a bit of ale with your eating?" he queried.

"No, Mr. Goodall, thank you just the same. I never drink."

"Don't like to mix good ale with your eating?"

"I never drink at all."

The farmer dropped his knife and fork in sheer amazement.

"So you are temperance. Well, well! you Americans are queer folks, I must allow."

"All our folks are not temperance, I can assure you of that," laughed Robert. "Some of them drink far more than is good for them."

"I've been used to my ale from childhood; I couldn't get along without it," answered the farmer, and then fell to eating, and Robert did the same.

The dinner finished, the two walked around to the railway station, and learned that they could get a train for Chishing in an hour and a half.

"I guess I had better spend the time in looking around for that thief," said Robert.

"Shall I go along?"

"If you wish to do so, Mr. Goodall."

"Yes, since I haven't anything else to occupy the wait with," answered the farmer.

But the hunt amounted to nothing, and ten minutes before train time the two reached the station again.

Promptly on time the train rolled in, and Robert and his friend entered one of the second-class coaches.

Luckily they were the only passengers, so to the boy it was quite like riding in a special car.

Had he had the money he would have purchased some books and newspapers with which to while away the time, but he did not care to make any further calls upon the farmer's generosity, so contented himself with gazing at the scenery along the road and in talking with his companion.

It was long after nightfall when they reached Chishing.

"You can settle up with me to-morrow," said Farmer Goodall. "I want to get home now and tell Dora how John got away," and so they separated.

It must be admitted that Robert's heart was heavy when he walked to the Cabe boarding house.

"I've made a bad mess of it," he told himself. "Perhaps Mrs. Vernon will not like it at all. Who knows but what she may discharge me for what has happened."

CHAPTER XXVI.
IN CHICAGO ONCE MORE.

Mrs. Vernon was sitting up waiting for Robert's return. She at once saw by his face that something was wrong.

"How did you get hurt?" she cried, as she noticed the court-plaster on his forehead.

"It's a long story, Mrs. Vernon," he answered, as he dropped into a chair. "I'm afraid you will be very angry when I tell you all."

"Why, Robert, what has happened?"

"I allowed your nephew to slip through my fingers."

"And that bruise on your head?"

"He did that. He knocked me senseless and robbed me of my watch, my pocketbook, and also that diamond scarfpin you gave me."

"And he has robbed me too," added the lady. "Robert, I am very sorry for you!" And she caught his hand.

"Robbed you!" he ejaculated. "You mean that check?"

"No, more than that. He took some of my jewelry the last time he visited me."

Again Robert had to tell his tale, and this time he related all of the details, for he felt that it would not do to hold back anything from the lady. She listened with her face growing whiter every instant.

"He is a terrible villain, Robert," she gasped at last. "So he did not sail for Australia, after all."

"No. I think he must be still hiding in Liverpool."

"Were it not for the scandal I would place a detective on his track. The attack on you was a most cowardly one."

"I don't believe he will worry either of us again very soon," said the boy. "He is too much afraid of arrest."

"He knows I am very indulgent," she sighed.

"Yes, but he knows he now has me to deal with as well as yourself, and he won't expect to find me so tender-hearted."

"That is true."

"If he shows his nose again I will make him give up what he stole and then threaten him with immediate arrest if he comes near us a second time," went on our hero warmly.

They figured up between them that Frederic Vernon, after disposing of the stolen things, would have about three thousand dollars in his possession.

"That will probably keep him for twelve months, since he used to expend that amount yearly," said Mrs. Vernon. "Oh, I sincerely trust I never see or hear of him again."

She promised to make good Robert's loss.

"I will buy you another scarfpin when we go back to London," she said, "and also another timepiece."

"The watch came from my father," answered Robert. "I would like to get it back if I could."

"We will notify the Liverpool police to search for it in the pawnshops."

On the next day Mr. Goodall received a call from Robert, who paid the farmer the money coming to him, and gave him a gift in addition.

"I shall not forget your kindness, Mr. Goodall," he said. "I trust some day I shall be able to do as much for you."

"Perhaps some day you'll meet my son John in America," replied the farmer. "If so, and you can give him a lift, that will please me more than anything else."

"I'll remember, if we ever do meet," said Robert.

The Liverpool police were notified, and inside of thirty-six hours the watch was recovered from a pawnbroker who had loaned two pounds on it. But the jewelry could not be traced.

Ten days passed, and then Mrs. Vernon received several additional letters from Chicago urging her to return home. Robert also received a very interesting letter from Livingston Palmer, but no communication from his mother, which disappointed him not a little.

"I would like to know how she and Mr. Talbot are getting along," he thought. "I hope he isn't making her any fresh troubles." He did not know that his mother had written, telling of her hard lot, and that Mr. Talbot had intercepted the communication and burnt it up.

"I think we had better sail for New York next Saturday, Robert," said Mrs. Vernon. "I do not wish to lose anything by not being in Chicago if my presence is required there."

"I am more than willing," he answered promptly.

"You do not like England then?"

"Oh, I can't say that. But I like the United States better."

"So do I, and that is natural, for both of us were born and brought up there."

Friday night found them in Liverpool, and here they engaged passage on one of the fastest transatlantic vessels running to New York. By Saturday afternoon they were well out on the ocean.

On the whole, the trip to England had done both Mrs. Vernon and Robert a good deal of good. Robert's face was round and ruddy, and he looked what he was fast becoming, a young man.

"They won't be able to call you a boy much longer," said Mrs. Vernon, during the trip. "I suppose you will soon be sporting a mustache." And she laughed.

"I guess I can wait a while for that," answered Robert. "But I won't mind if people think you have a young man for a secretary, instead of a boy. Some folks don't like to trust their business with a boy."

"I am perfectly willing to trust you, Robert."

"A man might have been smarter in Liverpool than I was."

"I don't think so. You were taken off your guard, and that might happen to anyone."

The voyage passed without special incident outside of a severe storm which was encountered on the third day out. During this storm all of the passengers had to remain below, and meals were served only under great difficulties.

"This is not so pleasant," observed Robert. "But I suppose we have got to take the bitter with the sweet."

"I shall be thankful if we don't go to the bottom," said Mrs. Vernon, with a shudder.

The storm lasted for twelve hours, and then departed as speedily as it had come, and the balance of the trip proved ideal, for at night there was a full moon, making the ocean look like one vast sheet of silver.

It was about four o'clock of an afternoon when they came in sight of New York harbor. From a distance they made out the statue of Liberty.

"Home again!" cried Robert. "I tell you there is nothing so good as the United States."

"Right you are, young man," replied a gentleman standing near. "I have traveled in many foreign countries, but give me the States every time."

They anchored at Quarantine over night, and landed at the pier ten o'clock the next morning. One day was spent in New York, and then they took the train for Chicago.

It made Robert's heart swell with delight to tread the familiar streets of Chicago once more. It seemed to him that he had been away a long time.

Mrs. Vernon had sent word ahead that she was coming, and at the depot a coach awaited her to take the lady and Robert to the handsome mansion of Prairie Avenue. Here Martha, the maid, met them at the door, her good-natured face wreathed in smiles.

"Welcome home again, Mrs. Vernon!" she cried joyfully. "And glad to see you, Master Robert."

"I am glad to be back," answered Mrs. Vernon.

Robert was soon back in his old room, and the expressman brought in the trunks. By night the youth was as much settled as he had ever been, and the same can be said of the lady who had made him her private secretary.

Mrs. Vernon's first move in the morning was to settle domestic affairs. Two days later Mr. Farley called upon her, and her next move was to attend a meeting of the stockholders of one of the companies in which she was interested.

"If you wish you can take a run home, Robert," she said, before going away.

"I thought, if you did not mind, I would go home over next Sunday," he replied.

"Then you can do that. But I shall not need you to-day."

"Then I'll take a walk downtown and see how matters look."

Before going out Robert wrote a long letter to his mother, telling of his adventures in England, and stating when he was coming home.

As he had done with the other letters, he marked this for Personal Delivery only, and sent it in care of the postmaster at Granville, that his step-father might not get hold of it.

His first call was at Mr. Gray's office, where he found Livingston Palmer behind the desk as usual.

"Right glad to see you, Robert," cried the clerk. "And I must thank you for that gift of yours."

"I trust you had a good time on your money, Livingston."

"Well, I didn't spend it foolishly, I can tell you that. I have learned a lesson, Robert. I am saving my spare money, and I am putting in most of my nights in learning stenography and typewriting. I have an offer of twenty-five dollars per week if I learn stenography thoroughly, and I am pegging away at it for all I am worth."

"I am glad to hear it," answered Robert heartily. "I have taken up stenography myself," and such was a fact.

The conversation lasted for quarter of an hour, and then our hero mentioned Dick Marden.

"Why, he is in town and at the Palmer House," said Livingston Palmer. "I saw him yesterday afternoon. You had better call on him. I know he will be glad to see you."

"I certainly will call on him, and at once," said Robert, and moved off without further delay.

CHAPTER XXVII.
DICK MARDEN'S GOOD NEWS.

On entering the Palmer House Robert was very much surprised to run across Dr. Remington.

At first glance he did not recognize the physician, for the latter's face was much bloated, showing that he had been drinking heavily, and his general appearance was seedy to the last degree.

"Why, hullo!" cried Dr. Remington, on seeing our hero. "When did you get back to Chicago?"

"I got back yesterday," replied Robert coldly. He was about to pass on when the doctor detained him.

"Got back yesterday, eh? Did you have a nice trip?"

"Yes."

"Glad to hear it, Frost. And how is Mrs. Vernon?"

"Very well."

"Good enough. I suppose an ocean trip was just what she wanted."

"It was," said Robert. He was struck with a sudden idea that perhaps Remington knew something of Frederic Vernon's whereabouts. "How have you been?"

"Oh, so so. You see, I've been troubled a good deal lately with the grippe."

"A doctor ought to be able to cure himself of that."

"So one would think, but it's pretty hard for a doctor to cure himself, even though he can cure others."

"How is your old friend Frederic Vernon these days?" went on our hero, in an apparently careless tone.

At this question Remington's face fell and took on a sour look.

"Vernon played me a mean trick," he muttered.

"How so?"

"Why, I--er--I loaned him some money, and he went off without paying me back."

"And you haven't seen anything of him since?"

"No. Do you know where he is?"

"I do not."

"Didn't he follow you to Europe?"

"He did. But he wasn't there long before he cleared out," added Robert.

By the manner in which Remington spoke he felt that the doctor had told the truth about Frederic Vernon, and if this was so it was likely that Vernon had not returned to Chicago.

"I'll wager he worried his aunt a good bit while he was there," went on Remington, closing one eye suggestively.

"He did. But I must go on, because I do not wish to miss meeting a friend of mine."

Robert tried to proceed, but again the seedy doctor detained him.

"Hold on a bit, Frost. I--er--that is, how are you fixed?"

"What do you mean?"

"Can you lend me ten dollars for a few days? I'm out trying to collect some bills from my patients, but all of them seem to be out of town."

This statement was a falsehood, for Remington had neither an office nor a practice left, and the few people that he did treat now and then had to pay him his small fee in spot cash.

"You will have to excuse me, Dr. Remington," said Robert. He saw no reason for accommodating the man who had caused his best friend so much trouble.

"Won't you lend me the money?" demanded the doctor half angrily.

"I will not."

"Don't get on a high-horse about it, Frost. Anybody is liable to get into a hole now and then."

"I am not getting on a high-horse. I don't care to lend you ten dollars, that's all."

"Then make it five. I'll pay you back to-morrow evening, sure."

"Dr. Remington, I shall not lend you five cents. I understand you, and I have no use for you. Now let me pass."

"You--you monkey!" hissed the irate doctor, and raised the cane he carried as if to strike Robert on the head. But the steady gaze out of our hero's eyes disconcerted him, and lowering the stick he passed on, and was soon swallowed up in the crowd on the street.

Robert found Dick Marden's room without trouble, and came upon the miner just as the latter was preparing to go away for the day.

"Robert, my boy!" cried Dick Marden, as he shook our hero's hand warmly. "I was just wondering if you were in Chicago or in England. You look well. How has it been with you?"

"All right, on the whole," answered the boy. "But I've had some strange adventures since I parted with you."

"Tell me about them."

The two sat down and Dick Marden listened with deep interest to all Robert had to relate.

"That Frederic Vernon is a bad one--a regular snake in the grass," he declared. "You want to beware of him."

"I intend to keep my eyes open."

"And you want to watch that Remington, too. Now Mrs. Vernon is back to Chicago the pair may try to do her further injury."

"But Remington says he doesn't know where Vernon is."

"Never mind, rogues always manage to get together again, no matter how they become separated, and they soon patch up their differences if there is any booty in sight. Do you know what I think that lady ought to do?"

"What?"

"Employ a detective as a sort of bodyguard. Then if that nephew and the doctor try any underhanded work the detective can catch them red-handed."

"I will suggest that to Mrs. Vernon."

"I suppose you would like to know how matters are going on at Timberville, Michigan."

"I would."

"Well, the news is first-rate. In the first place my uncle, Felix Amberton, is as well as ever again."

"I am very glad to hear that."

"In the second place his lawyers have made it so warm for those Canadians and Englishmen that were trying to defraud my uncle out of his timber lands, that the foreigners have given up the contest."

"They have left Mr. Amberton in sole possession of the lands?"

"Exactly. That map you procured from old Herman Wenrich did the business."

"In that case I don't think Mr. Wenrich ought to be forgotten by your uncle."

"My uncle has sent Herman Wenrich his check for one thousand dollars."

"That's nice. I am certain it will help Mr. Wenrich and his daughter Nettie a good deal, for they are not very well off."

"My uncle also thinks that you ought to be rewarded for your trouble," continued the miner. "He told me that as soon as you returned to America he was going to place a thousand dollars in the bank to your credit."

"A thousand dollars!" ejaculated Robert. "What for?"

"For what you did for him."

"I didn't do so much."

"He thinks you did, and so do I. You had lots of trouble in getting that map, and lots of trouble in delivering it after you got it."

"But a thousand dollars!"

"My uncle can easily afford it, for the timber lands are worth fifty times that amount."

"I am getting rich," mused Robert. "Do you know how much Mrs. Vernon has given me?"

"I haven't the least idea."

"When we were in England she placed two thousand dollars in the bank to my credit. The money will be transferred to a Chicago bank in a few days."

"That will make three thousand dollars. You are doing well, Robert, but you deserve it. You have had no easy time of it, to defend Mrs. Vernon against that unscrupulous nephew of hers."

"I hardly think he will dare bother me again. He knows that I can have him locked up for the assault on me."

"What do you intend to do with your money?"

"I am going to let it rest in the bank for the present, until I see some good investment. I am adding a little to it every month from my salary."

"I am glad to see you haven't turned spendthrift, Robert," said Marden warmly. "Many a young fellow would have his head turned by so much good fortune."

"Well, I'll try to keep my head--and my money, too," rejoined the youth, with a laugh.

A pleasant talk lasting quarter of an hour followed, and then Marden said he would have to go.

"But you must call on me again, Robert," he said, as they parted. "Remember, I consider you very largely my boy still."

"And you must call on me," added our hero warmly. "I am sure Mrs. Vernon will be pleased to have you do so."

"I am going up to Timberville in a day or two, and I'll tell my uncle you are back. You will probably get a letter from him by the beginning of next week," concluded the miner.

CHAPTER XXVIII.
IN WHICH MRS. VERNON IS MISSING.

Robert reached home about one o'clock, which was the usual hour that Mrs. Vernon and himself had lunch. He found the lady had not yet returned.

"I am in no hurry, Martha," he said. "I will go into the office and write some letters."

The letters took nearly an hour to finish, and by that time our hero felt decidedly hungry. Mrs. Vernon had told him never to wait over half an hour for a meal, so he now ordered lunch for himself alone.

"That meeting probably took longer than expected," he thought. "Perhaps she is having a whole lot of trouble with the other stockholders. I wish I could help her."

Slowly the afternoon wore away, and still Mrs. Vernon did not put in an appearance. Robert went out for another walk, and did not come back until six o'clock, the regular dinner hour.

"Not back yet, Martha?" was his first question, on returning.

"No, Mr. Frost."

"It is queer."

"Shall I have dinner served?"

"No, I will wait half an hour."

"It's too bad. The roast will be overdone, I am afraid."

"Well, it probably cannot be helped."

Robert drifted into the library, and selecting a volume of Cooper's works, sat down in an easy chair to read. But he could not fasten his attention on the story, and soon cast the volume aside.

"Is it possible that anything has happened to Mrs. Vernon?" was the question which he asked himself over and over again.

He thought of Frederic Vernon and Dr. Remington, and of what Dick Marden had said.

"Would Frederic Vernon dare to do anything?" he asked himself.

The evening passed slowly and painfully. As hour after hour went by Robert began to pace the floor nervously. He felt "in his bones," as the saying is, that something was wrong, but he could not exactly imagine what.

When the clock struck eleven he could stand the suspense no longer. He summoned Martha.

"I am going out to look for Mrs. Vernon," he said. "If she comes in in the meantime tell her not to worry about me."

"Very well," answered the maid.

Robert had decided to call first at the Masonic Temple, a large business building situated in the heart of Chicago. It was in the Temple that the offices were located which Mrs. Vernon had started to visit early that morning.

He rode the greater part of the distance and reached the office building shortly before midnight. The ground floor was still open, but the great majority of the offices were dark.

Approaching one of the hallmen he asked about the meeting of the manufacturing company.

"I don't know anything about that," was the answer. "But Joe Dolan does. I'll call him."

"The meeting broke up about noon," said Joe Dolan, when summoned.

"Do you remember Mrs. Vernon?"

"I don't know the lady by name. How was she dressed?"

As well as he was able, Robert described the lady's appearance.

"Oh, yes, I know her now," cried Joe Dolan. "There were only two ladies, you see, and the other was short and stout."

"Well, what became of Mrs. Vernon?"

"She went out ahead of the others."

"Alone?"

"Yes."

"Do you know what direction she took?"

"I do not."

"Are you sure she did not come back?"

"I didn't see anything of her, and I've been around ever since."

"Are the offices locked up?"

"Yes, and have been ever since five o'clock. No one but Mr. Smith has been in them since three o'clock."

"Then she must certainly have gone somewhere else."

"Do you calculate there is anything wrong?" said the janitor, with interest.

"I don't know what to think. She said she would return home from here, and she hadn't got back up to eleven o'clock."

"That looks bad."

"Of course something else may have come up that is keeping her away."

"That is so."

Thanking the janitor for his information, Robert left the Masonic Temple and walked up the street. He scarcely knew what to do next.

He would have called upon Mr. Farley for advice, but knew that the lawyer's offices were closed, and he had not the man's home address.

Hoping that Mrs. Vernon had returned to the mansion on Prairie Avenue, he returned. It was now nearly one o'clock, and it must be confessed that Robert was sleepy.

Martha had gone to bed, but William the butler sat dozing in a hall chair.

"No, she isn't home yet," said the butler, in reply to our hero's question. "I never knew her to stay out so late before, excepting when she went to a ball or something like that."

"There is something wrong, that is certain," said Robert. "I have half a mind to call on the police for aid."

"Better wait, Mr. Frost. It may be all right, and if the police were called in the newspapers might make a big sensation of it. And you know how much Mrs. Vernon dislikes scandals." The butler did not mention Frederic Vernon's doings, but he had them in mind, and Robert understood.

Our hero slept but little that night, and was up and dressed long before the usual breakfast hour. He passed to Mrs. Vernon's apartments, to find them still empty.

"I will go down to Mr. Farley's and have a talk with him," he told himself, and left the house in time to reach the lawyer's offices at nine o'clock--for he knew Mr. Farley would not be there earlier.

"This is certainly strange, Frost," said the lawyer, with a grave look on his face.

"I don't like it at all."

"Nor I, especially as I saw that nephew of hers in town yesterday morning."

"What, Frederic Vernon?"

"Yes."

"Then he is to blame for his aunt's disappearance," said Robert bitterly.

"What makes you think that?"

"I may as well tell you the truth, Mr. Farley, although I trust you will let the thing go no further. I believe you do not know exactly what reasons Mrs. Vernon had for going to England so suddenly."

"I know she had some trouble with her nephew."

"Frederic Vernon was plotting to put her into an insane asylum."

"You don't mean it, Frost!" gasped the lawyer.

"I do mean it. He had his plans all arranged, when I got wind of it, told Mrs. Vernon, and she left, without letting her nephew know anything about it."

"In that case, Frederic Vernon must be accountable for her present disappearance."

"I am half of a mind that that is so. The thing of it is, to catch the young man and prove it."

"That is so."

"If we catch him he may deny everything, unless he is certain he can make out a case of insanity against her."

"But she is no more insane than you or I!" cried Mr. Farley.

"I agree with you. But Frederic Vernon had a tool, a certain Dr. Remington, who was willing to swear that Mrs. Vernon was of unsound mind."

"It is a dastardly plot, and the man who invented it ought to be in prison."

"Mrs. Vernon hated publicity or anything in the nature of a family scandal. That is why she suffered so much in silence."

"We ought to find this Frederic Vernon at once."

"That is so."

"If you agree with me, we will put a private detective on his track. I know a reliable man, who knows when to talk and when to keep his mouth shut."

"Then that is the man to get. It would be foolish to allow Mrs. Vernon's enemies more time than necessary. They may be carrying her off to a great distance."

Mr. Farley was quick to act, and soon he and Robert were on the way to the place where Detective Brossom could be found.

As much as was necessary was told to the detective, and he was given a description of Frederic Vernon and also a list of the resorts which the spendthrift had been in the habit of frequenting.

"If he's in Chicago I'll run him down all right enough," said Brossom. "If I am not mistaken I've met him at one of the clubs, when I was running down Carew the bank wrecker."

"Of course we may be mistaken, and Mrs. Vernon may return home to-day," said Robert. "If she does, I will send word to this place immediately."

CHAPTER XXIX.
DOCTOR RUSHWOOD'S SANITARIUM.

Mrs. Vernon's house was built in the shape of a letter L, the lady's wing containing the library and business office downstairs and private apartments on the second floor.

When Robert let himself into the house he entered the library to find out if the lady had yet returned.

Nothing was disturbed, and he was about to walk into the business office, when on looking out on the street he saw Frederic Vernon standing behind a nearby tree, watching the mansion closely.

"Hullo," cried Robert to himself. "What is he up to now?"

At first he thought to go out and hail Vernon, but quickly changed his mind.

"I'll get nothing out of him by questioning him," he reasoned. "It will pay far better to watch him and see what he does and where he goes."

A few minutes after our hero had discovered Vernon, he saw the spendthrift hurry swiftly for the wing of the house and try the window to the business office.

The sash was locked, but by inserting a knife blade between the upper and lower sashes he was enabled to push the catch back.

This done the lower sash was raised, and Frederic Vernon crawled into the business office as silently as a cat.

"He is up to no good," said our hero to himself. "I believe he is here to steal something."

There was a large Turkish chair handy, and Robert crouched behind this, that Frederic Vernon might not see him should he take a peep into the library.

"Don't seem to be anybody around," he heard Vernon mutter, as he looked into the library. "Frost must be off trying to hunt the old woman up."

Vernon tiptoed his way to Mrs. Vernon's desk, and, unlocking it, slid back the roller top.

The movement surprised Robert, for he had thought that only Mrs. Vernon and himself had keys to the desk.

"Perhaps he is using Mrs. Vernon's key," he thought.

With great rapidity Frederic Vernon went through several drawers full of papers.

"Pshaw! The papers must be in the safe," he murmured, and leaving the desk he approached the safe, which stood in a corner. Getting down on his knees he began to work at the combination.

"Thirty-five twice, twelve three times," he murmured, repeating what had once been the combination of the lock.

But Mrs. Vernon had had Robert to change the combination just before starting for England, and consequently Frederic Vernon failed to get the door open.

He fussed with the combination for a quarter of an hour, getting more angry over his failure every minute.

"Confound the luck, they must have changed it," he muttered. "I wish I dared to tackle Frost about it. But I am not quite ready for that. Perhaps I can make her give me the combination."

Robert did not hear the last words, yet he felt pretty certain that Frederic Vernon was responsible for his aunt's disappearance, and knew where she was.

He was half of a mind to call in a policeman, yet he was afraid that Vernon might in some manner give the officer of the law the slip.

"And if he is locked up now he may deny knowing anything about his aunt," was the boy's conclusion.

At last Vernon left the safe and went to the desk once more. Here he selected several papers and rammed them in his pocket. Then, without warning, he slipped out of the window again, closed the sash, and started down the street at a brisk pace.

"I'll follow him," said Robert to himself. "And I won't leave him out of sight until I've found out what has become of Mrs. Vernon."

Running into the upper hallway Robert saw on a rack an old overcoat he had once worn and a slouch hat which had belonged to another inmate of the mansion.

He donned these, pulling the hat far down over his forehead, and the coat up around his neck. Then he put on a pair of blue glasses which Mrs. Vernon had used on the sea voyage to protect her eyes from the glare of the sun on the water.

Thus partially disguised, he made after Frederic Vernon, who had now reached the block below the house.

Here Vernon took a passing car and took a seat inside.

Running rapidly, Robert managed to catch the car, and took a position on the rear platform, with his back to the interior, that the young spendthrift might not see his face.

The car was one running well on toward the southern outskirts of Chicago, and Vernon remained in it until the very end of the line was gained.

Then he walked on once more, with Robert still dogging his footsteps, but so carefully that the young man never suspected he was being followed. Once he looked back, but our hero promptly stepped out of sight behind a nearby billboard.

In this district the houses were much scattered, and most of them were surrounded by large gardens.

Frederic Vernon passed into a side street which was little better than a road, and soon reached a large square building of stone, set in a perfect wilderness of trees and bushes. A high iron fence surrounded the ill-kept garden, and the single iron gate was locked.

Ringing a bell at the gate, Frederic Vernon thus summoned a porter, who came, and after asking him a few questions, let him in.

Approaching the gate, Robert saw a sign over it, in gilt letters, which read in this fashion:

Dr. Nicholas Rushwood,
Private Sanitarium for the Weak-Minded.

Peering through the ironwork, our hero saw Frederic Vernon follow the porter up the steps of the stone building and disappear inside.

"This must be the place to which Mrs. Vernon has been taken," thought Robert.

He waited at the gate for awhile to see if Frederic Vernon would come out, but the young spendthrift failed to put in an appearance.

The sanitarium was located on a corner, and ran from one street to the next, so that our hero could walk around three sides of the place. On the other side was a high stone wall, which separated the asylum grounds from those of a well-kept garden.

All of the windows on the second and third stories of the stone building were very closely barred.

"They must keep the patients up there," concluded Robert.

He gazed sharply at each window, but though he saw several men and women, he did not catch sight of Mrs. Vernon.

Presently a butcher boy came along the back street, a large basket on his arm.

"Can you tell me what place this is?" questioned Robert.

"That's Dr. Rushwood's asylum for crazy folks," answered the butcher boy.

"Has he many patients?"

"Ten or a dozen, I believe."

"Were you ever inside of the place?"

"I used to deliver meat there. But our firm don't serve him any more."

"And what kind of a place is it?"

"It's a gloomy hole, and the doctor is a terror."

"A terror? What do you mean by that?"

"He's awfully strict and awfully mean. Some folks say he don't give the crazy folks half enough to eat. He was always kicking about his meat bill. That's the reason our firm stopped serving him."

"Did you see them taking anybody new into there lately?"

"No, but I heard Jack Mason telling that he saw them taking a woman in there last night."

"A young woman or an elderly lady?"

"Jack said it was an oldish-looking woman, and said she was very handsomely dressed."

"What time was this?"

"About six o'clock last night. They brought her in a coach, and two men were with her. But what do you ask all these questions for?"

"I have my reasons. A lady has disappeared and I am looking for her."

"Christopher! Did they abduct her?"

"I don't know. I am much obliged to you," returned Robert, and to avoid being questioned further he sauntered off. He did not go far, however, and as soon as the butcher boy was gone, he returned to the vicinity of the sanitarium.

It was now growing dusk, and watching his chance he climbed to the top of the stone wall which divided the asylum grounds from that of the garden next door. The top of the wall was rough, but with care he managed to walk from one end to the other.

While he was on the wall he heard the gate bell ring, and crouched down to get out of sight. The porter admitted two men, but who they were Robert could not see.

From the wall Robert could easily look into the lower windows of the building. One room into which he gazed was fitted up as a library, and as he gazed into it the door opened and four men entered.

The four men were Frederic Vernon, Dr. Remington, and two others, the keeper of the asylum and a second physician.

CHAPTER XXX.
FREDERIC VERNON'S DEMANDS.

The window to the room was closed so that Robert could not hear what the four men said.

He, however, saw them talking earnestly, and then saw one of the strangers, probably the doctor who ran the asylum, bring out a legal-looking document. This Frederic Vernon urged Dr. Remington and the second stranger to sign.

"It must be the certificate to prove that Mrs. Vernon is insane," thought Robert. "I believe such a document has to be signed by two doctors, and Frederic Vernon is urging Remington and that other physician to do the dirty work for him." Robert's surmise was correct, as later events proved.

Remington did not wish to give the certificate until he was certain that Frederic Vernon would pay over the ten thousand dollars which had been promised to him.

"I've got to have my pay," he said, in a low but earnest manner.

"You'll get it," returned Vernon. "You can trust me."

"Humph! I trusted you before," growled the doctor.

"Well, you know why I went off--merely to induce my aunt to return to Chicago."

"Your money will be safe."

"And how about my money?" put in the second physician.

"You shall be paid, Dr. Carraway."

"You must remember that it is a ticklish business, this signing a certificate when the party isn't--ahem--just as bad as she might be."

"And I must have my money," put in Dr. Rushwood. "I am running a risk, too."

"What risk will you run if you have your certificate?" questioned Frederic Vernon. "You can fall back on that in case of trouble."

"Mrs. Vernon's friends may have us all arrested for conspiracy. It's a big risk."

"Well, every man of you shall be paid," said Frederic Vernon. "As soon as the excitement of the affair blows over, I'll take charge of all my aunt's property and then I'll have money to burn, and lots of it. Why, she's worth half a million."

So the talk ran on, until Dr. Remington and Dr. Carraway agreed to sign the certificate, and did so. This paper was then turned over to Dr. Rushwood, who placed it on file in his safe. Following this the keeper of the asylum brought out some wine and cigars, and half an hour was spent in general conversation.

Then Frederic Vernon said he would like to talk to his aunt for awhile.

Dr. Rushwood led the way to an apartment on the third floor. The room had once been well furnished, but the furnishings were now dilapidated, the carpet being worn threadbare and the furniture being scratched and broken. One small window lit up the apartment, and this was closely barred.

Frederic Vernon knocked on the door, but received no answer.

"Can I come in, aunt?" asked the young spendthrift.

At once there was a rustle in the room.

"Yes, Frederic, come in," came in Mrs. Vernon's voice.

Dr. Rushwood opened the door and the young man entered. Then the doctor locked the door again.

"When you want to get out just call me," he said significantly, and walked away.

"Frederic, what does this mean?" demanded Mrs. Vernon. By her face it was plain to see that she had been weeping.

"Don't excite yourself, aunt," responded the young rascal soothingly. "It is all for the best."

"What is for the best?" demanded the lady.

"That you are here."

"But I do not wish to be here, and you have no right to place me here."

"It is for your good, aunt."

"I understand you, Frederic, but let me tell you your wicked plot against me shall not succeed."

"I have no plot against you, aunt. If you wish to know the truth, let me tell you that your mind is not just what it should be. For a long while you have imagined that I was your enemy, while all your friends know that I have been your best friend."

"Indeed! Were you my friend when you forged my name to that check for six hundred dollars?"

Frederic Vernon winced, but quickly recovered.

"You do me a great injustice when you say I forged your name. I was never guilty of any such baseness."

"I know better."

"That is only another proof of your hallucination, aunt. But the doctor says if you will submit to his treatment you will be quite cured in a few months."

"I need no treatment, for my mind is as clear as yours, perhaps clearer. I want you and those wicked men who helped place me here to let me go."

"Such a course is impossible, and you must make yourself content with your surroundings. The room is not furnished as nicely as you may wish, but I will have all that changed in a day or two, as soon as I can get my other affairs straightened out."

"You will profit nothing by your high-handed course, Frederic. In the past I have been very indulgent toward you, but if you insist upon keeping me here against my will, when once I do get free I will let the law take its course."

The lady spoke so sharply and positively that Frederic Vernon was made to feel decidedly uncomfortable. He had carried matters with a high hand, and he realized that should the game go against him, the reckoning would be a bitter one.

"I would let you go, aunt, but I am certain I am acting for your own good. And now I want to talk business to you."

"If you do not give me my freedom I do not wish to say another word," answered the lady shortly.

"You must give me the combination of your safe."

"So that you can rob me again, eh? No, I will do nothing of the sort."

Frederic Vernon's face grew dark.

"You had better not defy me, aunt. I am bound to have the combination sooner or later."

"You will not get from me. Nor from Robert, either, I am thinking."

"I will get it somehow."

"Will you send Robert or Mr. Farley to me?"

"I cannot do that--just yet."

"Why not--if you are honest in your actions toward me?"

"Because it is against the doctor's orders. He says you must remain very quiet. It is the only hope of restoring you to your full mental health again."

"Very well then, Frederic. But remember what I said. If I ever get away again you shall suffer the full penalty of the law."

"You won't give me that combination?"

"No."

Mrs. Vernon remained obdurate, and a little while later the young man called Dr. Rushwood.

"You must be careful and watch her closely," said Frederic Vernon to the keeper of the asylum, as the pair walked downstairs. "She is clever, and will try to get the best of you if she can."

Dr. Rushwood smiled grimly.

"Don't worry about me, Vernon," he replied. "I've never yet had one of them to get the best of me."

"I am afraid it will take several days to break her down. At present I can do nothing with her."

"Perhaps I had better put her on a diet of bread and water. That sometimes fetches them," suggested the keeper of the asylum brutally.

"I am afraid she may do something desperate. She is a nervous, high-strung woman, remember."

"I've had all kinds to deal with, and I never miss it in judging them. You just leave the whole thing to me. When will you come again?"

"That must depend upon circumstances. Perhaps to-morrow afternoon."

"Will you take charge of her affairs at once?"

"I must feel my way before I do that. You see my aunt had a private secretary. He is nothing but a boy, but he may cause us a lot of trouble."

"Better discharge him at once, then, and make him turn over all his private business to you."

"That is what I intend to do."

"You said something about getting the combination of her safe."

"She wouldn't give it to me. But it won't matter so much. I can get an expert to open the safe--after I have sent that private secretary about his business," concluded Frederic Vernon.

CHAPTER XXXI.
ROBERT DECIDES TO ACT.

To go back to Robert at the time he was watching the four men in the room on the ground floor of the sanitarium.

Our hero saw the certificate signed, and a little later saw Dr. Remington and his friend arise to depart.

He leaped from the fence and ran around to the front of the grounds, and was just in time to see Remington and his companion stalk off in the direction of the nearest street car.

At first he thought to have the pair arrested, but on second thought concluded to wait. He must first have positive proof that Mrs. Vernon had been brought to the place, and that these men were implicated in the plot against the lady.

"It's one thing to know a truth," thought Robert. "It's another thing to prove it. I must wait until I can prove what I suspect."

After the two men had gone the youth walked around to the rear of the institution once more.

Some trees hid the upper windows from view, and to get a better sight of these Robert climbed one of the trees to the very top.

From this point he could look into several apartments.

The sight in one made his heart sick. On a bed lay an old man, reduced to almost a skeleton. The old man had his fists doubled up, and seemed to be fighting off some imaginary foe.

The next window was dark, and our hero turned to the third.

The sight that met his gaze here startled him. In a chair near the narrow window sat Mrs. Vernon, while in the center of the apartment stood her graceless nephew.

The conversation between the pair has already been given. Robert could not hear what was being said, but he saw every action, and saw that Mrs. Vernon was pleading to be released.

When Frederic Vernon went below, our hero slid down the tree and ran once more to the front of the house.

He saw Vernon come out and start for the street car line. It was now dark, and he managed to keep quite close to the young man without being discovered.

Now that he had seen Mrs. Vernon, Robert's mind was made up as to what he should do.

Frederic Vernon had to wait several minutes for a car. When it came along he hurried to a forward seat and gave himself up to his thoughts. As before, Robert kept on the rear platform.

The center of the city being reached, Frederic Vernon left the car and took his way to a leading hotel. Watching him, Robert saw the young man get a key from the night clerk and enter the elevator.

As soon as Vernon was out of sight Robert entered the hotel office and asked if he might look over the register.

"Certainly," answered the clerk.

Our hero soon found the entry, "Frederic Vernon, Chicago," and after it the number of his room--643.

"Mr. Vernon is stopping here, I see," he said to the clerk.

"Yes, he just went up to his room. Do you want to see him?"

"I won't bother him to-night, thank you," rejoined Robert, and walked out.

He felt pretty certain that Frederic Vernon had retired for the night, but in order to make certain he hung around for the best part of an hour. As Vernon did not re-appear he concluded that the young man had gone to bed.

"Now to find Mr. Farley and explain everything to him," said Robert.

In looking over the directory he found a long list of people by that name, and of this list three were lawyers.

Which of the three could be the man he was after was the question.

"I'll have to go it blind," said our hero to himself, and called a passing hack.

Soon he was on his way to the nearest of the three residences of the lawyers who bore the same family name. When he arrived he found a rather tumbled-down looking place. Telling the hackman to wait for him, he ran up the steps and rang the bell.

No answer was returned and he rang again. Presently an upper window was thrown up, and a head thrust out.

"What's wanted?" asked a deep bass voice.

"I am looking for Mr. Farley, the lawyer," answered Robert.

"All right, I'm your man."

"Hardly," thought Robert.

"I mean Mr. Farley who has his office in the Phoenix Building," he went on, aloud.

"Oh!" came the disappointed grunt. "I am not the fellow."

"So I see. Will you please tell me where he lives?"

"Somewhere out on Michigan Avenue. I don't remember the number." And with this the upper window was closed with a bang.

"That man doesn't believe in being accommodating," said Robert to himself. "However, there is no telling how many times he has been bothered by people looking for other Farleys."

He had the address of the Farley living on Michigan Avenue, and told the hackman to drive to it. The distance was covered in quarter of an hour. A sleepy-looking servant answered our hero's summons.

"Is Mr. Farley at home?"

"He is, but he went to bed long ago."

"Will you tell him that Robert Frost is here and wishes to see him on important business?"

"Yes, sir."

Robert was ushered into a library and the servant went off. Soon Mr. Farley appeared, in dressing gown and slippers.

"Why, Frost, what brings you here this time of night?" he asked, as he came in.

"I suppose you are surprised, Mr. Farley, but something quite out of the ordinary has happened, and I want your advice."

"I will assuredly do the best I can for you. What is the trouble?"

"Frederic Vernon has carried off Mrs. Vernon and had her placed in an asylum for the insane."

The lawyer emitted a low whistle.

"Is it possible!" he ejaculated.

"It is, sir. I hunted for Mrs. Vernon for several hours, and just located her a little while ago. She is confined in Dr. Rushwood's Sanitarium for the Weak-Minded, as the institution is called."

"I have heard of the place, and, let me add, Dr. Rushwood's reputation is none of the best."

"How Frederic Vernon got her there is still a mystery to me, but she is there, and I am pretty certain that he has got his tool, Dr. Remington, and another physician to certify that she is insane."

At this announcement the lawyer's face fell.

"In that case we may have considerable trouble in procuring her release."

"But she is no more insane than you or I."

"That is true, and I presume an examination in court will prove the fact."

"I can testify that Frederic Vernon plotted this whole thing out with Dr. Remington, and offered the doctor ten thousand dollars for his assistance."

"That will be good evidence in Mrs. Vernon's favor."

"We can prove, too, that Vernon forged his aunt's name to a check for six hundred dollars."

"Yes, I know that. I saw the forged check myself."

"And we can prove that he followed her to England and tried to take her life," added Robert. And then he told the particulars of the perilous carriage ride along the cliff and of how Frederic Vernon had been caught by Farmer Parsons.

"I guess we'll have a pretty clear case against that young man," said Mr. Farley, after Robert had finished.

Our hero then told of his following Frederic Vernon from Mrs. Vernon's mansion, and of what he had seen while hanging around Dr. Rushwood's institution.

"We ought to rescue Mrs. Vernon at once," he concluded. "If we don't Frederic Vernon may take it into his head to do her harm."

"I think we had better have Vernon and Dr. Remington arrested first," answered the lawyer.

He returned to his room above and donned his street clothing. A little later he and Robert were driven to the office of the private detective who had been engaged to hunt up Frederic Vernon.

"He is around town," said Brossom. "I've seen him. He is thick again with that Dr. Remington." He had learned a few things, but was astonished when Robert told his tale.

"Why, you ought to be a detective yourself, young man," he cried.

"Thanks, but I don't care for the work," was our hero's dry response.

Brossom agreed that it would be best to arrest Frederic Vernon without delay. The arrests of Dr. Remington and the other physician could then follow.

Again the hack was called into service, and they proceeded to the hotel at which Frederic Vernon had been stopping since his return to the city by the Great Lakes.

"I will see Mr. Vernon now, if you please," said Robert.

"Sorry, but Mr. Vernon went out about half an hour ago," was the clerk's answer, which filled our hero with dismay.

CHAPTER XXXII.
THE BEGINNING OF THE END.

"Gone!"

"Yes, sir."

"Did he say where to?"

"He did not."

"Did he say he would be back?"

"No, he said nothing, just handed over his key and went off as fast as he could."

Our hero turned to the lawyer.

"What do you make of this?" he asked.

"Perhaps he has gone to the asylum," suggested Mr. Farley.

"Or to Mrs. Vernon's residence," put in the detective.

"He may have gone to rejoin Dr. Remington and that other physician," said Robert.

The three talked the matter over for some time, but could reach no satisfactory conclusion regarding Frederic Vernon's departure from the hotel.

"I think it will be best to take the bull by the horns, and have Mrs. Vernon released without delay," said the detective. "Unless we do that her nephew may get it into his head to have her taken a long distance off."

This was thought good advice, and leaving the hotel they told the hackman to drive them to Dr. Rushwood's Sanitarium.

"Sure an' I'm havin' a long spell av it," grinned the Jehu.

"So you are," answered Robert. "But you shall be fully paid for your work."

"Is somethin' wrong?"

"Very much wrong, and we are going to set it right."

"Thin Mike Grady is wid yez to the end," said the hack driver, as he slammed shut the door of his turnout.

When they reached the asylum they saw that all of the lower rooms were dark. In two of the upper apartments lights were burning.

"Come around and I will show you the room in which Mrs. Vernon is confined," said our hero.

They walked to the rear of the institution and Robert pointed up through the tree at the window.

As they looked up Mrs. Vernon's face appeared from behind the bars.

"There she is!" cried Robert. "I wish I could attract her attention."

He decided to climb the tree again, and aided by the detective he went up with all possible speed.

One branch grew closer to the window than the others, and Robert went out on this as far as he dared. Then he waved his handkerchief.

Even in the darkness the white object fluttering in the wind attracted Mrs. Vernon's attention, and she looked intently in the direction.

At last she recognized Robert, and her face showed her joy. She had had the window shut to exclude the cool night air, but now she raised the sash.

"Robert!" she cried softly. "Oh, how glad I am that you have come!"

"Don't speak too loudly, Mrs. Vernon, or they may hear you."

"Are you alone?"

"No, Mr. Farley is below, and also a private detective."

"Thank God for that. You have come to save me, of course."

"Yes. Is anybody around, or have they all gone to bed?"

"I have seen nobody since my nephew was here several hours ago."

"I wish I could get to the window, I would soon have those bars out and get in to help you," went on Robert, after a pause.

"Never mind, tell Mr. Farley and the detective to go around to the front door and demand admittance."

Robert descended to the ground and repeated what the lady had said.

The men and our hero walked to the great iron gate and rang the bell.

Nobody answered the summons.

"We had better climb the fence and try the front door," said Brossom.

"I'm afraid I am not equal to it," answered Mr. Farley, as he surveyed the iron barrier dubiously.

"There is an easy way to get into the garden from the rear end of that dividing wall," said Robert, pointing out the wall in question. "Come along."

The spot was soon gained, and the boy leaped up on the wall. Mr. Farley came next, and the detective followed. They picked their way through the tangled shrubbery, and ascending the piazza rang the bell loudly.

The bark of a dog rang out, and then they heard hasty footsteps sound through the hallway.

"Who is there?" came in a high-pitched voice.

"I wish to see Dr. Rushwood on important business," answered Mr. Farley. "Let me in at once."

"Wait till I call the doctor," was the reply.

The dog continued to bark and to rattle his chain. A few minutes passed, and then Dr. Rushwood put in appearance.

"Wha--what is the meaning of this?" he stammered, as he found himself confronted by three people, when he had expected to see only one person.

"We have important business with you, Dr. Rushwood," replied Mr. Farley, as he forced his way into the hall, followed by the detective and Robert.

"What is your business?"

"You have a lady confined here--Mrs. Vernon."

The keeper of the asylum changed color and fell back a step.

"Well--er--what do you want?" he stammered.

"We want you to release the lady at once."

"But she is confined here as a--a person of--of weak mind."

"She is all right, and you know it," put in Robert. "If you try to make any trouble for us it will go hard with you, I can promise you that."

"And who are you to threaten me?" demanded Dr. Rushwood.

"I am Robert Frost, Mrs. Vernon's private secretary. Mrs. Vernon has been confined here through a plot hatched out by her worthless nephew, Frederic Vernon, and his tool, Dr. Remington."

"The young man tells the truth," put in Mr. Farley. "If you wish to keep out of trouble you will make us no trouble."

"And you are----?" faltered Rushwood.

"I am Louis Farley, the lawyer."

"And I am Frank Brossom, the detective," put in that individual. "Doctor, the game is up, and you had better retire as gracefully as you can."

"Retire?" thundered Dr. Rushwood, who felt that he must put on a front. "I have done nothing of which I am ashamed. The lady is here on the certificate of two doctors. If anything is wrong----"

"You will right it, of course," finished the detective, thus affording Rushwood a loop-hole through which he might escape. "Very well, take us up to the lady."

"Of course I will right anything that is wrong."

"Then take us up to Mrs. Vernon," put in Robert, and started for the stairs.

"See here, it seems to me that you are very forward," blustered the doctor.

"I shall not waste time with you," answered Robert. "I know where Mrs. Vernon is, and I am going up to her," and he began to ascend the stairs.

"Be careful, young man, or I may loosen my dog."

"If you do he'll be a dead animal in about two seconds," answered Brossom.

Robert ran up to the third floor of the house, and speedily found Mrs. Vernon's room.

Luckily the key to the door was on a nearby peg, and he quickly took it down and let himself into the apartment.

The lady was waiting for him, and almost threw herself into his sturdy arms.

"Robert!" she cried. "Oh, what a friend you have proved to be!"

Mr. Farley followed our hero, and then came the doctor and the detective.

Dr. Rushwood felt that the game was indeed up, and to save himself insisted that he had been imposed upon.

"I told the other doctors that Mrs. Vernon did not act like a very crazy person," he said. "But they assured me that she was in the habit of having violent spells."

Robert assisted Mrs. Vernon down to the lower floor and then a servant was called upon to unlock the gate leading to the road.

The hack was in waiting, and without listening to any more Dr. Rushwood might have to say, the party got in and were driven directly for Mrs. Vernon's mansion.

Here it was decided that Robert should remain with Mrs. Vernon until morning, while Mr. Farley returned home and the detective went on a hunt for Frederic Vernon and his accomplices.

Mrs. Vernon was very nervous because of her bitter experience, and had Robert occupy a room next to her own, while William the butler was requested to do his sleeping on a couch in the hall.

It must be confessed that our hero slept but little during the remainder of the night. His thoughts were busy concerning the rescue and what Frederic Vernon would do next. He was exceedingly thankful that he had been able to render such signal service to the lady who had been so much of a friend to him.

On the following morning Mr. Farley put in an appearance, and steps were taken to proceed against Frederic Vernon and those who had aided him in his wicked plot against his aunt. But these steps proved of no avail, for, later on, it was discovered that the rascally nephew had taken a lake steamer to Canada. From Canada Frederic Vernon drifted to the West, and then joined a gold hunting party bound for Alaska. He was caught in a blizzard while out among the mines, and was so badly frozen that recovery was impossible. He sent word to his aunt, telling of his condition, and she forwarded sufficient money for him to return to Chicago. Here he lingered in a hospital for several months, and then died. Before his death he professed to be very sorry for his many wrong-doings, and told where he had pawned the balance of the jewelry he had stolen, and the articles were eventually recovered.

Dr. Remington also disappeared, as did Dr. Carraway, and what ever became of them Robert never learned.

CHAPTER XXXIII.
ROBERT'S HEROISM--CONCLUSION.

It took several days to straighten matters out around the Vernon household, and so Robert's proposed visit home had to be deferred until the middle of the week following.

Mrs. Vernon was truly grateful to the youth for all he had done, and did not hesitate to declare that she was going to make him her principal heir when she died.

"You did nobly, Robert," she said. "Your mother should be proud of you. No woman could have a better son."

As Frederic Vernon had disappeared, the scandal was hushed up, the detective paid off, and there the matter was allowed to drop. This was a great relief to Dr. Rushwood, who had dreaded an exposure. But exposure soon came through another so-styled patient, and the doctor had to depart in a great hurry, which he did, leaving a great number of unpaid bills behind him.

One day came a letter for Robert, which made him feel very sober. It was from his mother.

> "I wish you would come home and assist me in my money affairs," wrote Mrs. Talbot. "Mr. Talbot had asked me for more than I am willing to lend him, and lately he has taken to drink and is making me very miserable."

"The wretch!" muttered Robert, when he had finished the communication. "What a pity mother ever threw herself away on such a man. I'll run home this very afternoon," and receiving permission from Mrs. Vernon he hurried up and caught the first train leaving after the lunch hour.

Robert had not been to Granville for a long time, and he felt rather strange as he stepped off the train. No one was at the depot to receive him, yet he met several people that he knew.

"Why if it aint Robert Frost!" cried Sam Jones, his old school chum. "How are you getting along, Robert? But there's no need to ask, by the nice clothes you are wearing."

"I am doing very well, Sam," replied our hero. "And how are you faring?"

"Pretty good. I am learning the carpenter's trade."

"I see."

"Come home to stay?"

"No, just to see my mother."

Sam Jones' face fell a little.

"It's too bad she's having such a hard time of it, Robert--indeed it is."

"So you know she is having a hard time?"

"Why, everybody in Granville knows it. Mr. Talbot is drinking like a fish, and using up her money fast, too, so they say."

"It's a shame," muttered Robert. "It's a wonder mother didn't write before."

"Going up to the house now?" continued Sam.

"Yes."

"You'll be in time for a jolly row. I just saw your step-father going up there, and he was about half full."

"It's too bad, Sam. I'll have to do the best I can. I wish my mother would come to Chicago and live with me."

The two boys separated, and our hero continued on his way to what had once been his happy home.

The main street of Granville was a winding one, and after running away from the railroad for a short distance, it crossed the tracks a second time and then led up a hill, on the top of which was built the Frost homestead.

As Robert approached the railroad he saw a familiar figure ahead of him, reeling from side to side of the dusty roadway. The figure was that of his step-father.

The sight filled him with disgust, and he did not know whether to stop and speak to the man or pass him by unnoticed.

While he was deliberating James Talbot reeled down to the railroad tracks, staggered, and fell headlong. He tried to rise, but the effort seemed a failure, and then he sank down in a drunken stupor.

"He is too drunk to walk any further," thought Robert. "Oh, what a beast he is making of himself! If he----"

Our hero broke off short, as the whistle of an approaching train reached his quick ears. The afternoon express was coming--along the very tracks upon which his step-father lay!

The boy's heart seemed to stop beating. The drunken man was unconscious of his danger--he could not help himself. Supposing he was left where he lay? There would be a rushing and crushing of heavy wheels, and then all would be over, and this man, who was not fit to live, would be removed from the Frost path forever!

This was the thought that came into Robert's mind, a thought born of the Evil One himself. But then came another thought, as piercing as a shaft of golden light, "Love your enemies." The boy dropped the valise he was carrying and leaped forward madly.

"Get up! get up!" he yelled, as he caught the drunken man by the arm. "Get up! The train is coming!"

"Whazzer mazzer!" hiccoughed James Talbot dreamily. "Lemme alone, I shay!"

"Get off the railroad track!" went on Robert. "The train is coming!"

"Train!" repeated the drunkard. "I--hic--don't shee no train."

But now the whistle sounded louder than ever, and around the turn of the hill appeared the locomotive of the express, speeding along at a rate of fifty-five miles an hour. The sight caused Robert's heart to thump loudly, while James Talbot gazed at the iron monster as though transfixed with terror.

"We're lost!" he screamed hoarsely, and then straightened out and sank back like one dead.

What happened in the next few seconds Robert could hardly tell in detail. He had a hazy recollection of catching his step-father by the leg and jerking him from the track and falling down on top of him. Man and boy rolled into a dry ditch, and as they went down the express thundered by, the engineer being unable to stop the heavy train short of twice its own length. And when Robert came to his senses he was lying on a grassy bank and Sam Jones and several others were bathing him with water.

"My step-father--is he saved?" were the youth's first words.

"Yes, he was saved," answered one of the men. "But he seems to be suffering from another stroke of paralysis."

Robert soon felt strong enough to get up, and asked for his valise, which was handed over to him. His brave deed had been witnessed by Sam Jones and a farmer who had been driving toward the railroad crossing. Both of these explained to the crowd how our hero had risked his life to save that of his intoxicated step-father.

A stretcher was procured and Mr. Talbot was placed upon this and carried to his home. The whole lower portion of his body seemed to be paralyzed and he spoke with great difficulty. Strange to say the shock had completely sobered him.

It was a strange meeting between Mrs. Talbot and Robert. Tears were in the eyes of the mother, tears which only her son understood. With great care James Talbot was carried to a bed-chamber on the second floor of the house and here made as comfortable as possible, while one of the neighbors went off to summon a doctor.

"They tell me you risked your life to save him," whispered Mrs. Talbot to Robert. "Oh, Robert, my boy! my only boy!" And she clasped him about the neck and burst into a passionate fit of weeping.

When the doctor had made a careful examination he looked very grave.

"The shock is a heavy one, Mrs. Talbot," he said. "And coming on top of that which he had some time ago, is likely to prove serious."

"Do you mean he will die?" she asked quickly.

"'While there is life there is hope,' that is all I can say," said the physician, and then gave directions as to what should be done for the sufferer.

In the morning James Talbot was no better, physically, although able to talk a little. From his wife he learned what Robert had done for him.

"He's a good boy," he whispered huskily. "A better boy than I am a man."

"James, when you get well you must give up drinking," she replied.

"I won't get well, Sarah--I feel it. But I won't drink any more, I promise you." And then she kissed him on the forehead. She had loved him once, and now, when he lay helpless, she could not help but love him again.

Two days later it was evident that the end was drawing near. Before this came he asked for his wife and told her to bring Robert. When the two were at his bedside he placed their hands one within the other.

"Robert, I'm going," he said slowly and painfully. "Will you forgive the past?"

"I will," answered Robert. His emotion was such that he could scarcely speak.

"And, Sarah, will you forgive me, too?" went on the dying man, turning his yearning eyes toward his wife.

"Oh, James, James, there is nothing to forgive!" she wailed, and fell on his bosom.

"I've done a good deal of wrong, and this is the end of it. Robert, be a good boy and take care of your mother, for she is the best woman in the world. I--I--wish--I had--been--better too. If I----"

James Talbot tried to say more, but could not. A spasm had seized him, and when it was over the paralysis had touched his tongue, and his speech was silenced forever. He died at sunset, and was buried on the Sunday following, in the little Granville cemetery where Robert's father rested.

The taking off of James Talbot made a great change in Robert's mother. She became a deep-thinking, serious woman, and from that hour on her heart and soul were wrapped up in her only child.

To get her away from the scene of her sorrows, Robert wrote to Mrs. Vernon, and that lady promptly invited the widow to pay her a visit, and this invitation was accepted. The two ladies soon became warm friends, and it was decided that in the future Mrs. Talbot was to spend her winters in Chicago, while each summer Mrs. Vernon and Robert should come to Granville for an outing.

"Because, you see," said Mrs. Vernon, "we'll have to divide Robert between us, since neither of us can very well give him up."

* * * * *

Several years have passed since the events recorded above took place. Robert has gone through a college education, and, in connection with Mr. Farley, manages all of Mrs. Vernon's business affairs for her. It is well known that he will be the rich lady's principal heir when she dies, but he openly declares that it is his hope she will live for many a long year to come.

Robert frequently hears from Dick Marden and from his old fellow clerk, Livingston Palmer. Through Marden Robert received a thousand dollars with the compliments of Felix Amberton. Both the lumberman and the miner are doing well. Livingston Palmer has mastered stenography thoroughly and is now Mr. Farley's private clerk, at a salary of thirty dollars per week. To use Palmer's own words, "this beats clerking in a cut-rate ticket office or traveling with a theatrical company all to pieces."

As yet Robert is unmarried. But he is a frequent visitor at the home of Herman Wenrich, and rumor has it that some day he will make pretty Nettie Wenrich his wife. He is interested in a number of business ventures of his own, and is fast becoming rich, but no matter what good luck may befall him, it is not likely that he will ever forget the thrilling adventures through which he passed when he was unconsciously Falling in with Fortune.